THE
FORBIDDEN

2: THE CHASE

She wanted to speak but she couldn't. She could only clutch the phone and listen.

"A isht..."

Damaged? No, that was even farther off. A-isht. Am-ish. Amished.

Oh my *God*. Oh God oh God oh God...

Sheer black terror swept through her, and every hair on her body erected. She felt her eyes go wide and tears spring to them. In that instant she heard, really heard what the voice was saying. She *knew*.

Not *vanished*. It sounded like *vanished,* but it wasn't. It was something much worse. The whispery, distorted voice with the odd cadence was saying *famished*.

Famished.

Jenny threw the phone as hard as she could across the room. She was on her feet, her skin crawling, body washed with adrenaline. *Famished. Famished.* The eyes in the closet. The Shadow Men.

Those evil, *ravenous* eyes...

The better to *eat* you with, my dear.

Look out for:

Halloween Night II
R.L. Stine

The Forbidden Game III:
The Kill
L.J. Smith

Nightmare Hall:
Guilty
Diane Hoh

Point Horror

THE FORBIDDEN GAME

2: THE CHASE

L.J. Smith

SCHOLASTIC

Scholastic Children's Books,
7-9 Pratt Street, London NW1 0AE, UK
a division of Scholastic Publications Ltd
London ~ New York ~ Toronto ~ Sydney ~ Auckland

First published in the US by Simon & Schuster Inc., 1994
First published in the UK by Scholastic Publications Ltd, 1995

Copyright © Lisa J. Smith, 1994

ISBN 0 590 13156 7

Printed by Cox and Wyman Ltd, Reading, Berks

10 9 8 7 6 5 4 3 2 1

*For Joanne Finucan, a true heroine
and lifelong inspiration*

1

It wasn't so much the hunting. It was the killing.

That was what brought Gordie Wilson out to the Santa Ana foothills on a sunny May morning like this. That was why he was cutting school even though he wasn't sure he'd get away with forging his mom's signature on another readmit. It wasn't the wild-flower-splashed hills, the sky blue lupines, or the fragrant purple sage. It was the wet, plopping sound when lead met flesh.

The kill.

Gordie preferred big game, but rabbits were always available—if you knew how to dodge the rangers. He'd never been caught yet.

He'd always liked killing. When he was seven, he'd gotten robins and starlings with his BB gun. When he was nine, it had been ground squirrels with a shotgun. Twelve, and his dad took him on a real hunting trip, going after white-tailed deer with an old .243 Winchester.

That had been so special. But then, every kill was special. It was like his dad said: *"Good hunts never end."* Every night in bed Gordie thought about the very best ones, remembering the stalking, the shooting, the electric moment of death. He even hunted in his dreams.

For one instant, as he made his way along the dry creek bed, a memory flickered at him, like a little tongue of flame. A nightmare. Just once Gordie had dreamed that he was on the other side of the rifle sights, the one with dogs snapping behind him, the one being hunted. A chase that had only ended when he woke up dripping sweat.

Stupid dream. He wasn't a rabbit, he was a hunter. Top of the food chain. He'd gotten a moose last year.

Big game like that was worth observing, studying, planning for. But not rabbits. Gordie just liked to come up here and kick them out of the bushes.

This was a good place. A sage-covered slope rising toward a stand of oak and sycamore trees, with some good brush piles underneath for cover. Bound to be a bunny under one of those.

Then he saw it. Right out in the open. Little desert cottontail sunning itself near a squat of grass. It was aware of him, but still. Frozen. Ter-*rif*-ic, Gordie thought. He knew how to sneak up on a rabbit, get so close he could practically catch it with bare hands.

The trick was to make the rabbit think you didn't see it. If you only looked at it sideways, if you walked kind of zigzag while slowly getting closer and closer . . .

As long as its ears stayed down, instead of up and swiveling, you were safe.

Gordie edged carefully around a lemonade berry

bush, looking out of the corner of his eye. He was so close now that he could see the rabbit's whiskers. Pure happiness filled him, warmth pooling in his stomach. It was going to hold still for him.

God, this was the exciting part, the *gooood* part. Breath held, he raised the rifle, centered the crosshairs. Got ready to gently squeeze the trigger.

There was an explosion of motion, a gray-brown blur and the flash of a white tail. It was getting away!

Gordie's rifle barked, but the slug struck the ground just behind the rabbit, kicking up dust. The rabbit bounded on, down into the dry creek bed, losing itself among the cattails.

Damn! He wished he'd brought a dog. Like his dad's beagle, Aggie. Dogs were crazy about the chase. Gordie loved to watch them do it, loved to draw it out, waiting for the dog to bring the rabbit around in a circle. It was a shame to end a good chase too soon. His dad sometimes let a rabbit go if it ran a good enough race, but that was crazy. What good was a hunt without the kill?

There were times when Gordie . . . wondered about himself.

He sensed vaguely that his hunting was somehow different than his dad's. He did things when he was alone that he never told anybody about. When he was five, he used to pour rubbing alcohol on earwigs. They'd writhed a long time before they died. Even now he would swerve to run over a possum or a cat in the road if he could.

Killing felt so good. Any kind of killing.

That was Gordie Wilson's little secret.

The bunny was gone. He'd spooked it. Or . . .

Maybe something else had.

A strange feeling was growing in Gordie. It had developed so slowly he hadn't even noticed when it started, and it was like nothing he'd ever felt before —at least awake. A . . . rabbit-feeling. Like what a rabbit might feel when it freezes, crouched down, with the hunter's eyes on it. Like what a squirrel might feel when it sees something big creeping slowly closer.

A . . . *watched* feeling.

The skin on the back of his neck began to crawl.

There were eyes watching him. He felt it with the part of his brain that hadn't changed in a hundred million years. The reptile part.

Gingerly, flesh still creeping, he turned.

Directly behind him three old sycamores grew close enough together to cast a shade. But the darkness underneath was too dark to be just a shadow. It was more like a black vapor hanging there.

Something was under those trees. Something else had been watching the rabbit.

Now it was watching him.

The black vapor seemed to stir. White teeth glinted out of the darkness, as bright as sunlight on water.

Gordie's eyes bulged in their sockets.

What the—what *was* it?

The vapor moved again and he saw.

Only—it couldn't be. It couldn't be what he thought he saw, because it—*just couldn't be.* Because there wasn't anything like that in the world, so it *just couldn't—*

It was beyond anything he'd ever imagined. When

4

it moved, it moved *fast*. Gordie got off one shot as it surged toward him. Then he turned and ran.

He went the way the rabbit had, slipping and slithering down the slope, tearing his jeans and his hands on prickly pear cactus. The thing he'd seen was right behind him. He could hear it breathing. His foot caught on a stone, and he fell heavily, arms flailing.

He rolled over and saw it in the full sunlight. His mouth sagged open. He tried to scoot away on his backside, but sheer terror paralyzed his muscles.

Deliberately it closed in.

A loose, blubbery wail came from Gordie's lips. His last wild thought was *Not me—not me—I'm not a rabbit—not meeeeee—*

His heart stopped before it even got its teeth in him.

Jenny was brushing her hair, *really* brushing it, feeling it crackle and lift by itself to meet the plastic bristles in the static electricity of this golden May afternoon. She gazed absently at her own reflection, seeing a girl with forest green eyes, dark as pine needles, and eyebrows that were straight, like two decisive brush strokes. The hair that lifted to meet the brush was the color of honey in sunlight.

"They didn't do it."

Jenny stopped abruptly. A girl was reflected behind her in the mirror.

The girl had dark hair and dark eyes reddened with crying. She looked poised for flight out of the bathroom.

"I'm sorry?"

5

"I said, they didn't *do* it. Slug and P.C. They didn't kill your friend Summer."

Oh. Jenny found herself gripping the brush hard, unable to even turn her head. She could only look at the girl's eyes reflected in the mirror, but she understood now. "I never said they did," she said softly and carefully. "I just told the police that they were around that night. And that they stole something from my living room. A paper house. A game."

"I *hate* you."

Shocked, Jenny turned.

"You and your preppy friends—*you* did it. You killed her yourselves. And someday everybody will know and you'll pay and you'll be sorry." The girl was twisting a Kleenex between slim olive-tan fingers, tearing it into little bits. Her long hair was absolutely straight except for the slight undersweep of the ends, and her dark eyes were pensive. She didn't belong at Vista Grande High; Jenny had never seen her before.

Jenny put the brush down and went to her, facing her directly. The girl looked taken aback.

"Why were you crying?" Jenny said gently.

"Why should you care? You're a soshe. You wear your fancy clothes to school and hang out with your rich friends—"

"Who's rich? What have my clothes got to do with it?" Jenny could feel her eyebrows come together. She looked pointedly at the girl's fashionably tattered designer jeans.

The girl spoke sullenly. "You're a soshe . . ."

Jenny grabbed her.

6

"I am not a soshe," she said fiercely. "I am a human being. So are you. So what is your problem?"

The girl wouldn't say anything. She twisted under Jenny's hands, and Jenny felt the small bones in her shoulders. Finally, almost spitting it in Jenny's face, she said, "P.C. was my friend. He never did anything to that girl. You and your friends did something, something so bad that you had to hide her body and tell those lies. But you just wait. I can prove P.C. didn't hurt her. I can *prove* it."

Despite the warm day, hairs rose on Jenny's arms. Her little fingers tingled.

"What do you mean?"

Something in her face must have scared the girl. "Never mind."

"No, you tell me. How could you prove it? Did you—"

"Let *go* of me!"

I'm being rough, Jenny realized. I'm never rough. But she couldn't seem to stop. Chills were sweeping over her, and she wanted to shake the information out of the girl.

"Did you see him or something?" she demanded. "Did he come home the next morning alone? Did you see what he did with the paper hou—"

Pain exploded against her shinbone. The girl had kicked her. Jenny lost her grip, and the girl wrenched away, running to the bathroom door.

"*Wait!* You don't understand—"

The girl jerked the door open and darted out. Jenny hopped after her, but by the time she looked up and down the second-story walkway, the girl was gone. There were only a few bits of twisted Kleenex on the concrete floor.

Jenny hobbled over to the nearest locker bay and looked into it. Nothing but students and lockers. Then she limped back and looked over the railing of the open walkway to the main courtyard. Nothing but students with lunches.

Young. The girl had been young, probably a ninth grader. Maybe she'd come from Magnolia Junior High. It was within walking distance.

Whoever she was, Jenny had to find her. Whoever she was, she'd seen something. She might *know* . . .

I left my purse in the bathroom, Jenny realized. She retrieved it and slowly walked back out.

The pay phone beside the bathroom was ringing. Jenny glanced around—two teachers were locking up a classroom, students were streaming down the stairs on each end of the building. Nobody seemed to be waiting for a call, nobody even seemed to notice the ringing.

Jenny lifted the receiver. "Hello," she said, feeling foolish.

She heard an electronic hiss, white noise. Then there was a click, and in the static she seemed to hear a low whispering in a male voice. It was distorted, drawn out, and there was something weird about the way the syllables were stressed. It sounded like one word whispered over and over.

A as in *amble*. Then a dragging, hissing sigh: *ish*. *A . . . ish . . .*

Gibberish.

"Hello?"

Shhshhshhshhshhshhshhshhshh. Click. In the background she heard something that might have been speech, a

8

sharp, staccato burst. Again, the rhythm was weird. It sounded like some *very* foreign language.

Bad connection, Jenny thought. She hung up.

Her little fingers were tingling again. But she didn't have time to think about it now. That girl had to be found.

I'd better get the others, Jenny thought.

2

She looked in on Tom's business law class first, but he wasn't there. She headed downstairs. Then she began to forge her way across campus, weaving around fellow students who were staking out their favorite benches. She could hear paper bags rustling and smell other peoples' lunches.

Jenny's group hadn't been eating together these last two weeks—it caused too much talk. But today they had no choice.

Audrey next, Jenny thought. She passed the amphitheater with its blistered wooden benches and looked into one of the home ec rooms. Audrey was taking interior decorating, and—of course—acing it.

Jenny just stood in the doorway until Audrey, who was lingering with the teacher, looked up and caught her eye. Audrey shut her folder, dropped it in her backpack, and came.

"What is it?"

"We've got to get everybody," Jenny said. "Do you have your lunch?"

"Yes." Audrey didn't ask why they had to get everybody. She just shook spiky copper bangs out of her eyes with an expert toss of her head and pressed her cherry-glossed lips together.

They cut across the center of campus toward the girls' gym. The sun shone on Jenny's head, sending a little trickle of dampness down the back of her neck. Too hot for May, even in California. So why did she feel so cold inside?

She and Audrey peered into the girls' locker room. Dee wasn't even dressed yet, snapping towels and snickering with a couple of girls on the swim team. She was naked and completely unself-conscious, beautiful and lithe and supple as a jet-black panther. When she saw Jenny and Audrey looking at her significantly, she hiked an eyebrow at them, then nodded. She reached for a garnet-colored T-shirt and joined them a minute later.

They found Zach in the art block, standing alone outside the photography lab. That wasn't surprising —Zach was usually alone. What surprised Jenny was that he wasn't *inside* the lab, working. Zach's thin, intense face had always been pale, but these days it looked almost chalky, and in the last few weeks he'd taken to wearing black cotton twills and shirts. He's changed, Jenny thought. Well, no wonder. What they'd been through would have changed anyone.

He saw Jenny, who tilted her head in the general direction of the staff parking lot. The usual place. He gave a brief jerk of his head that meant agreement. He'd meet them there.

They found Michael near the English block, picking up scattered papers and books from the concrete floor.

"Jerks, porkers, bozos, *Neanderthals,*" he was muttering.

"Who did it?" Jenny asked as Audrey checked Michael for bruises.

"Carl Vortman and Steve Matsushima." Michael's round face was flushed and his dark hair even more rumpled than usual. "It would help if you kissed it *here,*" he said to Audrey, pointing to the corner of his mouth.

Dee did a swift, flowing punch-and-kick to the air that looked like dancing. "I'll take care of them," she said, flashing her most barbaric smile.

"Come on, we've got to talk," Jenny said. "Has anybody seen Tom?"

"I think he cut this morning," Audrey said. "He wasn't in history or English."

Wonderful, Jenny thought as Michael got his lunch. Zachary was wearing Morbid Black, Michael was getting stomped, and Tom, the super-student, was cutting whole mornings—just when she needed him most.

They sat down by the parking lot on what was commonly known at Vista Grande High as the grassy knoll. Zach arrived and dropped first his lunch sack, then himself to the ground, folding his long, thin legs in one easy motion.

"What's happening?" Dee said.

Jenny took a deep breath.

"There's this girl," she said, and she did her best to describe the Crying Girl. "Probably a ninth grader," she said. "Do any of you guys know her?"

They all shook their heads.

"Because she said *we* killed Summer and hid her body, and that she knew that P.C. didn't do it. She sounded like somebody who really did know, and not just because she has faith in him or something."

Dee's sloe-black eyes were narrowed. "You think—"

"I think maybe she saw him that morning. And that means—"

"Maybe she knows where the paper house is," Michael said, looking more alarmed than excited.

"If she does, we have to find her," Jenny said.

Michael groaned.

Jenny didn't blame him. Everything about their situation was awful. The way people looked at them now, the questions in people's eyes—and the danger. The danger that no one but their group knew about.

A lot of it was Jenny's fault. It had been her own brilliant idea. *Let's tell the police the truth. . . .*

There were two policewomen. One was Hawaiian or Polynesian and model-beautiful. The other was a stocky motherly person. They both examined the pile of fragments around the sliding glass door.

"But that doesn't have anything to *do* with Summer," Jenny said, and then she and Tom and Michael and Audrey explained it all again.

No, it hadn't been a UFO. Well, it had been sort of like a UFO—Julian was *alien,* all right, but he hadn't broken the door. He had come out of a game—or at least he had sucked them *into* a game. Or at least—

All right. From the beginning again.

Jenny had bought the game on Montevideo Avenue, in a store called More Games. Okay? She'd bought it and brought it home and they had all

13

opened it. Yes, they'd all been here, the six of them, plus Summer. It had been a party for Tom's seventeenth birthday.

Inside had been this cardboard house. This model. They had put it together, a Victorian house, three stories and a turret. Blue.

Then they'd put these paper dolls inside that they'd colored to look like themselves. Yeah, right, they *were* a little old to be playing with paper dolls. But it wasn't just a dollhouse. It was a game.

The game was to draw your worst nightmare and put it in a room of the house, and then, starting at the bottom, work your way up to the top. Going through each different person's nightmare as you went.

It had seemed like a good game. Only then it turned real.

Yes, real. *Real.* How many different ways were there to say real? *Real!*

They had all sort of passed out, and when they woke up, they were in the house. Inside it. It wasn't cardboard anymore. It was solid, like an ordinary house. Then Julian had showed up.

Who was Julian? *What* was Julian, that was the question. If you thought of him as a demon prince, you wouldn't be too far off. He called himself the Shadow Man.

The Shadow Man. Like the Sandman, only he brings nightmares.

Look, the point was that Julian had killed Summer. He made her face her worst nightmare, which was a messy room. Piles of garbage and giant cockroaches. Yes, it did sound funny, but it wasn't. . . .

No, none of them had read Kafka.

Look, it wasn't funny because it had *killed* Sum-

14

mer. She'd been buried in a garbage dump from hell, under piles of filth and rotting stuff. They'd heard her screaming and screaming, and then finally the screaming had stopped.

The body? For God's sake, where else would the body be? It was *there,* buried in rubbish, in the paper house, in the Shadow World.

No! The sliding glass door did not have anything to do with it. That had happened after they escaped from the Shadow World. Jenny had tricked Julian and locked him behind a door with a rune of constraint on it. When they got back to the real world, Jenny had put the paper house back in the game box, and then they'd called the police. Yes, that was the call made at 6:34 this morning. While they were on the phone, they'd heard glass breaking and come out to see two guys taking the box over the back fence.

Why would anybody want to steal the box? Well, these guys had been following Jenny when she bought the Game. And seeing the Game—it did something to you. Once you saw that glossy white box, you wanted it, no matter what. The guys had probably followed Jenny home just to get the box.

NO, SUMMER DIDN'T GO THAT WAY, TOO! SUMMER WASN'T THERE! SUMMER WAS AL-READY DEAD BY THEN!

It was only after telling it that Jenny saw how crazy the story sounded. At first the police wouldn't believe that Summer was *really* missing, no matter how many times Tom demanded a lie detector test.

The police finally began to believe when they called Summer's parents and found that nobody had seen her since last night. By then Jenny and the others were sitting in the detective bureau around a large table with detectives' desks all around them. By then Jenny had picked out pictures of the two guys who'd stolen the game. P.C. Serrani and Scott Martell, better known as Slug, a name he'd chosen himself. They both had records for shoplifting and joyriding. P.C. was the one who'd been wearing the bandanna and black leather vest, Slug the one in the flannels with the bad complexion.

And it turned out that they were both missing, too.

The worst part was when Summer's parents came down to the station to ask Jenny where Summer really was. They didn't understand why Jenny, who had known Summer since fourth grade, wouldn't tell them the truth now. The kids finally were given a drug-screening test because Summer's father insisted their story sounded exactly like things he'd seen in the sixties. Like a very, very bad trip.

Mrs. Parker-Pearson kept saying, "Whatever Summer's done, it doesn't matter. Just tell us where she is."

It was *horrible.*

Aba was the one who finally stopped it.

Just at the point when the fuss got the biggest and noisiest, she appeared. She was wearing a brilliant orange garment that was more like a robe than a dress, and an orange headcloth like a turban. She was Dee's grandmother, but she looked like visiting royalty. She asked the police to leave her alone with the children.

Then Jenny, shaking all over, told the story again. From the beginning.

When it was over, she looked at each of them. At

Tom, the champion athlete, sitting with his normally neat dark hair wildly tousled. At Audrey, the ever-chic, with her mascara rubbed off from sobbing. At Zach, the unshakable photographer, whose gray eyes were glassy with shock. At Michael, with his rumpled head in his arms. At Dee, the only one of them still sitting up straight, proud and tense and *furious,* her hair glistening like mica with sweat.

At Jenny, who had looked back at her with a mute plea for understanding.

Then Aba looked down at her own interlaced fingers, sculptor's fingers, long and beautiful even if they were knotted with age.

"I've told you a lot of stories," she said to Jenny, "but there's a famous one I don't think you've heard. It's a Hausa story. My ancestors were those-who-speak-Hausa, you know, and my mother told me this when I was just a little girl."

Michael slowly lifted his head from the table.

"Once there was a hunter who went out into the bush, and he found a skull lying on the ground. He said, although he was really speaking to himself, 'Why, how did you get here?'

"To his astonishment, the skull answered, 'I got here through talking, my friend.' "

Tom leaned forward, listening. Audrey stared. She didn't know Aba as well as the rest of them.

Aba went right on. "The hunter was very excited. He ran back to his village and told everyone that he had seen a talking skull. When the chief of the village heard, he asked the hunter to take him to the marvelous skull.

"So the hunter took the chief to the skull. 'Talk,' he

said, but the skull just lay there. The chief was so angry at being tricked that he cut off the hunter's head and left it lying on the ground.

"Once the chief was gone, the skull said to the severed head beside it, 'Why, how did you get here?' And the head replied, 'I got here through talking, my friend!'"

In the long silence afterward, Jenny could hear distant telephones ringing and voices outside the room.

"You mean," Michael said finally, "that we've been talking too much?"

"I mean that you don't need to tell *everything* you know to *everyone*. There is a time to be silent. Also, you don't have to insist that your view is the only one, even if you honestly believe it. That hunter might have lived if he'd said, 'I think a skull talked to me, but I may have dreamed it.'"

"But we didn't dream it," Jenny whispered.

What Aba said then made all the difference. It made everything easier somehow.

"I believe you," she said quietly and laid a gentle, knotted hand on Jenny's.

When the police came back, everyone was calm. Jenny's group now admitted that while they thought they were telling the truth, it could have been some sort of dream or hallucination. The police now theorized that something really *had* happened to Summer, something so awful that the kids just couldn't accept what they'd seen, and so had made up a hysterical story to cover the memory. Teenagers were especially prone to mass hallucination, Inspector Somebody explained to Aba. If they could pass a lie detector test, proving they hadn't done anything to Summer . . .

They passed.

Then the police released them into the custody of their parents, and Jenny went home and slept for sixteen hours straight. When she woke up, it was Sunday and Summer was still missing. So were Slug and P.C.

That was how the Center got started.

The new idea was that Slug and P.C. had made off with Summer, or that someone else had made off with all three. The local shopping mall donated space for a search center. Hundreds of volunteers went out looking in stormpipes and ditches and Dumpsters.

There was nothing Jenny could do to stop any of it. Every day the volunteers did more, the search got bigger.

She felt awful. But then she realized something.

Summer's body wasn't in a Dumpster—but the paper house might be. It wouldn't do any good searching for Summer, but it might do some good to search for Slug and P.C.

"Because," she pointed out bleakly to Dee and the others, "they got into the paper house, all right. And that means they might get up to the third floor. And *that* means they might open a certain door and let Julian out. . . ."

After that they went out every day with the other volunteers, looking for a clue to where Slug Martell and P.C. Serrani might have taken the Game. It was a race against time, Jenny thought. To get to the house before Slug and P.C. got to Julian. Because after what she had done to Julian, tricking him and locking him behind that door, and after what she had promised him—telling him she'd stay with him forever—and then running away . . .

If he ever got out, he would find her. He'd hunt her down. And he'd take his revenge.

3

On the grassy knoll Michael was still groaning at the thought of finding the Crying Girl.

"She probably doesn't know anything," Zach said, his eyes gray as winter clouds. "She probably just wonders if maybe we did it. Deep down, I think everybody wonders."

Jenny looked around at the group: Dee sprawled lazily on the grass, dark limbs gleaming; Audrey perched on a folder to save her white tuxedo pantsuit; Michael with his teddy-bear body and sarcastic spaniel eyes; and Zach sitting like some kind of Tibetan monk with a ponytail. They didn't look like murderers. But what Zach was saying was true, and it was just like him to say it.

"We've got to go postering today anyway," Audrey said. "We might as well look for this girl while we're at it."

"It's not going to make any difference," Zach said flatly.

The others turned to Jenny. He's your cousin; you deal with him, their looks said.

Jenny took another deep breath. "You know perfectly well it *will* make a difference," she said tightly. "If we don't get the paper house back—you *know* what could happen."

"And what are you going to do if we *do* get it? Burn it? Shred it? With them inside? Isn't *that* murder, or don't P.C. and Slug count?"

Everyone burst into speech. "They wouldn't care about us—" Audrey began.

"Just cool it," Dee said, standing over Zach like a lioness.

"Maybe they're not inside. Maybe they just took it and skipped town or something," Michael offered.

Jenny gathered all her self-control, then she stood, looking at Zach directly. "If you don't have anything useful to say, then you'd better leave," she said.

She saw the looks of surprise from the others. Zach didn't look surprised. He stood, his thin beaky-nosed face even more intense than usual, staring at Jenny. Then, without a word, he turned around and left.

Jenny sat back down, feeling shaken.

"Good grief," Michael said mildly.

"He deserved it," said Dee.

Jenny knew the point was not whether Zach had deserved it, but that Michael was surprised Jenny would give it to him.

I've changed, Jenny thought. She tried to push the knowledge away with a "So what," but it nagged at her. She had the feeling that, deep down, she might have changed more than anybody knew yet.

"We have to find the paper house," she said.

"Right," Dee said. "Even though I don't think

there's a chance in hell of P.C. and Slug making it all the way to the third floor where Julian is. Not with that snake and that wolf around—"

"The Creeper and the Lurker," Audrey said with precision.

"—but we might as well be safe." A bell rang. "See you in physiology," Dee added to Jenny, grabbed her empty Carbo-Force can, and ran for the art block.

Michael brushed cookie crumbs off his lap, got up, and began the trek to the gym.

Jenny knew she should be hurrying, too. She and Audrey had to get changed for tennis. But at the moment she really didn't care if she was late or not.

"Want to cut?" she said to Audrey.

Audrey stopped dead in the middle of reapplying her lipstick. Then she finished, snapped her compact shut, and put the lipstick away. "What's *happened* to you?" she said.

"Nothing—" Jenny was beginning, when she realized that somebody was walking up to them.

It was a guy, a senior from Jenny's world lit class. Brian Dettlinger. He looked at Audrey uncertainly, but when it was apparent she wasn't going anywhere he said hi to both of them.

Jenny and Audrey said hi back.

"Just wondering," he said, eyeing a bumblebee hovering over a clump of Mexican lilies, "if you had, you know, a date for the prom."

Prom's over, Jenny thought stupidly. Then she realized that of course he meant senior prom.

Audrey's chestnut eyes had widened. "No, she doesn't," she said instantly, with the slight pursing of lips that brought out her beauty mark.

"But I have a *boyfriend*," Jenny said, astonished.

Everyone knew that. Just as everyone knew that she and Tom had been together since elementary school, that for years people had talked about them as Tom-and-Jenny, a single unit, as if they were joined at the hip. Everyone *knew* that.

"Oh, yeah," Brian Dettlinger said, looking vaguely embarrassed. "But I just thought—he isn't around much anymore, and . . ."

"Thank you," Jenny said. "I can't go." She knew she sounded scandalized, and that Brian didn't deserve it. He was only trying to be nice. But she was put off balance by the whole situation. Obviously she couldn't have been his first choice, since today was Monday and the prom was this Saturday, but to have been asked at all by him was a compliment. Brian Dettlinger wasn't just any scabby senior scrambling for a date at the last minute, he was captain of the football team and went with the head cheerleader. He was a star.

"Ma è pazzo?" Audrey said when he'd gone. "Are you nuts? That was *Brian Dettlinger.*"

"What did you expect me to do? Go with him?"

"No—well—" Audrey shook her head, then tilted it backward, to look at Jenny appraisingly through spiky jet-black lashes. "You *have* changed, you know. It's almost scary. It's like you've blossomed, and everybody's noticed. Like a light went on inside you. Ever since—"

"We have to go to P.E.," Jenny said abruptly.

"I thought you wanted to cut."

"Not anymore." Jenny didn't want anything else to change. She wanted to be safe, the way she was before. She wanted to be a regular junior looking forward to summer vacation in a month or so. She wanted Tom.

"Come on," she said. For a moment, just as they left, dropping iced tea bottles in the metal trash can by the English block, she had the feeling that someone was watching her. She turned her head quickly, but she couldn't see anything there.

Tom watched her go.

He felt bad lurking there in the shadow of the English building, behind the scarred metal pillars that held the porchlike roof up. But he couldn't make himself come out.

He was going to lose her, and it was his own fault.

The thing was, he'd blown it already. He'd screwed up. The most important thing in his life—and he hadn't even realized it was the most important thing until seventeen days ago. April 22. The day of the Game. The day Julian came and took Jenny away.

Of course he'd *loved* Jenny. Loving was easy. But he'd never thought about what it might feel like without her, because he'd always known she'd be there. You don't sit around and think to yourself, "I wonder what it would feel like if the sun didn't come up tomorrow."

He'd assumed things, taken things for granted. He'd been lazy. That was what came of having everything handed to you on a platter. Of never having to prove yourself, of having people fawn on you because of your good looks and your hot car and your knuckleball. Of, essentially, being Tom Locke. You get to think you don't *need* anything.

Then you find out how wrong you are.

The problem was that just when he'd started to realize how much he needed Jenny Thornton, she'd discovered she didn't need him.

He'd *seen* her in that Other Place, inside that paper house that had turned real. She'd been so brave and so beautiful it made his throat hurt. She'd functioned absolutely perfectly without him.

It might still have been all right—except for Julian. The Shadow Man. The guy with eyes the color of glacier pools, the guy that had kidnapped all of them because he wanted Jenny. Which had been an indisputably evil, but in Tom's view, completely understandable thing to do.

Jenny had changed since Julian had gotten to her. Maybe the others hadn't really noticed yet, but Tom had. She was different now, even more beautiful, and just—different. There were times when she sat with a faraway look as if she were listening to things no one else could hear. Listening to Julian's voice in her mind, maybe.

Because Julian had loved her. Julian had said it, had said all the things that Tom had never thought to mention. And Julian had the charm of the devil.

How could Jenny resist that? Especially being as innocent as she was. Jenny might actually think that she could change Julian, or that he wasn't as evil as he seemed. Tom knew differently, but what was the use of telling her? He'd seen them together, seen Julian's eyes when he looked at her. He'd seen the kind of spell Julian could cast. When Julian came for Jenny next time, Tom was going to lose.

So now all he could do was lurk in shadows, watching her. Noticing the way wisps of her hair blew over the rest of it, light as cornsilk and the color of honey in sunlight. Remembering her eyes, a dark green touched with gold. Everything about her was golden, even her skin. Funny he'd never bothered to tell her that. Maybe that was what Dettlinger had been doing just now. Tom wasn't surprised that the football star had come to talk with Jenny; he was just surprised at how fast he'd gone away. He wished he could have heard the conversation.

It didn't matter. It didn't matter how many guys approached Jenny. Tom was only worried about one—and that one had better watch out.

Tom couldn't have her anymore, but he could protect her. When Julian did come back—not *if*; Tom was virtually certain that he would—*when* Julian did come back for Jenny, and tried to play on her innocence again, Tom would be there to stop it. He didn't quite know how, but he *would* stop it.

Even if it killed him.

And if it made Jenny hate him, so be it. She'd thank him someday.

Moving quietly and purposefully, Tom followed the copper head and the golden one, stalking the girls to the gym.

It might have been his imagination, but he had the odd feeling that something else was stalking them, too.

They drove to the Center in two cars; Jenny and Audrey in Audrey's little red Alpha Spider, and Dee and Michael in Michael's VW Bug. Jenny braced herself as they walked inside.

No matter how she braced, the west wall was still a shock. It was covered with pictures of Summer.

Hundreds of them. Not just the flyers and posters.

Summer's parents had brought in dozens of photographs, too, to show Summer from different angles, or maybe just to remind people what all this efficiency and envelope-stuffing was really about. Somebody had gotten one of the pictures blown up into a monstrous billboard-like print, so that Summer's soft blond curls spanned five feet and Summer's wisteria blue eyes stared out at them like God's.

"Where's the Tomcat?" one of the volunteers asked Jenny. She was a college girl, and she always asked about Tom.

"I don't know," Jenny said briefly. The same question had been stabbing at her since lunch.

"If I were you, *I'd* know. What a hunk. I'd be keeping tabs on him. . . ." Jenny stopped listening. As usual, she wanted to get away from the Center as soon as possible. It was a warm, earnest, busy place, full of hope and good cheer—and it was a farce.

There was a sick feeling in Jenny's stomach as she turned to the large map on the wall. The map showed which areas had been postered and which hadn't. Jenny pretended to study it, even though she already knew where she had to go. If the Crying Girl had been P.C.'s friend, she might live near him.

She scarcely noticed as the Center door opened and one of the volunteers whispered, "It's that psychic who called. The one from Beverly Hills."

"Will you look at that Mercedes?" Michael said.

Jenny turned and saw a woman with frosted blond hair, who was decorated with ropes of expensive-looking gold chains. At the same moment the psychic turned and saw *her*—and gasped.

Her eyes got very large. She took several steps toward Jenny, until her Giorgio perfume overpowered Audrey's Chloé Narcisse. She stared into Jenny's face.

"You," she whispered, "have seen them. Those from the Other Side."

Jenny stood frozen. Lightning-struck.

"I have a message for you," the psychic said.

4

What message?" Dee said, frowning.

The psychic was still staring at Jenny intently. "You've got the look," she said. "You've seen *them* —the faery folk."

Audrey said sharply, "The faery folk?" In the paper house Audrey's worst nightmare had been a fairy tale. A story about the Erlking, a spirit who haunted the Black Forest and stole children. The Elf-king. Julian had played the part to perfection, had even claimed to be the *real* Erlking.

The Shadow Men. The faery folk. Different names for different ages. Oh, God, Jenny thought, she knows the truth. I should be happy, she thought wildly. But there was a knot in her stomach.

The woman was answering Audrey. "The Elder Race. Some people have the gift of seeing them where everyone else only sees a wind in the grass, or a shadow, or a reflection of light."

Something about the woman's tone brought Jenny

up short. The psychic sounded too—pleased—about the subject. Not scared enough. "What do they look like?"

The woman gave her a laughing glance. *As if you didn't know.* "They're the most beautiful things imaginable," she said. "Creatures of light and happiness. I frequently see them dancing at Malibu Creek." She held up one of her chains, and Jenny saw the charm, a beautiful young girl with gauzy wings and floating draperies.

"Pixies in bluebells," Dee said, absolutely straight-faced. Jenny's muscles went slack. This woman didn't know anything about the Shadow Men. Just another kook.

The psychic was still smiling. "The message is: *Vanished.* They told me to tell you that."

"Vanished? Oh," Jenny said. "Well, thank you." She supposed it was as good a message as any, considering Summer's situation.

"Vanished," the woman repeated. "At least—I *think* that was it. Sometimes I only get the vowel sounds. It might have been—" She hesitated, then shook her head and went back to her Mercedes.

"For a moment there I thought she had something," Audrey murmured.

Jenny grabbed a handful of flyers and a map. "Let's go."

Outside, they made their plans. "P.C.'s house is at thirteen-twenty-two Ramona Street," Jenny said. She knew this by heart. It was the first place they had checked, along with Slug's house. Of course, they hadn't been able to search directly, but one of the kinder detectives had let them know that there was no paper house in either of the boys' homes.

"Dee, you and Michael can start there and cover everything west over to, say, Anchor Street. Audrey and I can cover everything east over to where Landana turns into Sycamore. Remember, it's the girl we want now."

"In other words we're canvassing the entire south side of town," Michael said with a groan. "Door to door."

"Obviously we won't cover it all today," Jenny said. "But we'll keep at it until we do." She looked at Dee, who nodded slightly. Dee would keep Michael at it.

Audrey didn't look particularly happy, either. "We've been to a lot of those houses before. What are we supposed to say when they tell us they already have flyers?"

Dee grinned. "Tell them you're selling encyclopedias." She hustled Michael into the Bug.

Audrey shook her head as she and Jenny got back into the Spider and drove away. The top was down, and the wind blew stray wisps of copper-colored hair out of her chignon. Jenny shut her eyes, feeling the rushing air on her face.

She didn't want to think about anything, not about the psychic, not about Zach, not about Tom. Especially not about Tom. Underneath she'd had some faint hope he might show up at the Center after school. He was avoiding her, that was it.

Her nose and eyes stung. She wanted him *with* her. If she thought any more about him, about his hazel eyes with their flecks of green, about his warmth and his strength and his easy devil-may-care smile, she was going to cry.

"Let's go over by Eastman and Montevideo," she

heard herself saying. The words just came out of her mouth, from nowhere.

Audrey cast her a spiky-lashed glance but turned south.

Eastman Avenue, the scene of so many recent riots, was almost deserted. Jenny hadn't been there since the day of Tom's birthday, the day she'd walked there to buy a party game. As they approached Montevideo Street, everything Jenny had experienced the last time she'd been here—the blue twilight, the footsteps behind her, the fear—came back to her. She almost expected to see P.C. in his black vest and Slug in his flannels walking down the sidewalk.

Audrey turned the corner on Montevideo and stopped.

The mural on the blank wall still showed a street scene. In the middle of the mural was a realistic-looking store with a sign reading: More Games. But it was just paint and concrete. Flat. There was no handle sticking out of the door.

Behind that blank wall she'd met Julian, in a place that wasn't a real place after all.

Scraps of paper lay in the street. One was the bright yellow of Summer's flyer.

Jenny felt suddenly very hollow. She didn't know what she'd expected to find here, or even what had made her come.

Audrey shivered. "I don't like this place."

"No. It was a bad idea."

They drove north, backtracking. They were actually near Summer's house now, in the kind of neighborhood where cars tended to be slightly dented, on blocks, or in pieces in the side yard. The afternoon seemed brighter here, and on the sidewalks the usual kids with sun-bleached hair and freckled limbs or night-black hair and brown limbs were running around.

They parked the car by George Washington Elementary School and put the top up.

At every house the spiel was the same.

"Hi, we're from the Summer Parker-Pearson Citizen's Search Committee. Can we give you a flyer . . . ?"

If the people in the house looked nice, they tried to get invited in. Then came the transition from "We're looking for Summer" to "We're looking for an important clue in her disappearance"—meaning the paper house. And today, "We're looking for somebody who might know something about her"—meaning the Crying Girl with the long dark hair and haunted eyes.

Most of all, though, they tried to talk to kids.

Kids knew things. Kids saw things. Usually the adults in the houses only listened politely, but the kids were always eager to help. They followed along on their bicycles, suggesting places to look, remembering that they thought they might have seen someone who could possibly have been Summer yesterday, or maybe it was the day before.

"The paper house is really important, but it could be dangerous. Anybody could have picked it up, thinking it was a toy," Jenny told one nine-year-old while Audrey kept his mother occupied. The nine-year-old nodded, his eyes bright and alert. Behind him, on a cracked leather sofa, a girl of four or five was sitting with a dog-eared book on her lap.

"That's Nori. She can't really read yet."

"I can, too." Tilting her face toward the book, although her eyes still remained on her brother, Nori said, "Then Little Red Riding Hood says, 'Grandma, what big *eyes* you have.' Then the wolf says, 'The better to *see* you with, my dear.'"

Jenny smiled at her, then turned back to the boy. "So if you see it or the white box, don't touch it, but call the number on the flyer and leave a message for me."

". . . Grandma, what big *ears* you have. . . ."

"I'll know what you mean if you say, 'I've found it.'"

The boy nodded again. He understood about things like clues and secret messages.

". . . The better to *hear* you with, my dear. . . ."

"Or if one of your friends knows about a girl with dark hair that was good friends with P.C. Serrani—"

". . . Grandma, what big *teeth* you have. . . ."

Audrey was finished with the mother. Jenny gave the boy a quick touch on the shoulder and turned to the door.

". . . *The better to EAT you with, my dear!*" Nori shrieked suddenly, bolting up on the couch. Jenny whirled—and dropped her flyers. Nori was standing, eyes wide, mouth pulled into a grimace. For an instant Jenny saw, not a child, but a small, misshapen goblin.

Then the mother cried, "Nori!" and Jenny was jerked back to reality. She felt herself turn red as she gathered the flyers.

Nori began to giggle. Jenny apologized. The mother scolded. Finally they got out of the house.

"I am *never* going to have children," Audrey said, outside.

They kept going. Some people were friendly, others were rude. A shirtless man laughed unkindly when they started the spiel about Summer and rasped, "Did you check the mall?" Almost all of them already had heard about the missing girl.

Dinnertime came and went. They called their parents to say they'd be out for a little longer, while it was still light.

Jenny glanced sideways at Audrey, a little surprised. Audrey wasn't the suffering-in-silence type. Jenny had expected to have to cajole her to stay out this long.

There was a lot more to Audrey than her glamour-magazine exterior let on.

They came to a street where a lot of kids were playing. Jenny recognized the white-blond head of the one covering his eyes against a tree. It was Summer's ten-year-old brother.

"Cam!" she said, startled. He didn't hear her. He went on counting, leaning on his folded arms. Other kids were scattering, hiding in open garages, behind bushes, in ivy. Jenny recognized two more of them. One was Dee's little sister, Kiah, the other was her own younger brother, Joey.

They came to play with Cam after dinner, she realized. It was a long way for Kiah, even on a bike.

"What are they playing?" Audrey asked.

"It looks like cops and robbers." At Audrey's blank expression Jenny remembered. Audrey had grown up in every place but America; her father was with the diplomatic corps. If he hadn't retired early, she wouldn't be in California now.

"It's a chase game. You capture the robbers and take them back to your home base as prisoners. Hey, watch out!" Jenny caught a small figure that had erupted out of the nearby ivy, tripped, and gone flying. It was Kiah, and Cam was close on her heels.

Kiah looked up. She was never going to be tall like Dee, but she had Dee's fine bones and wild, leaping beauty. Cam had hair like dandelion fluff, even lighter than Summer's. It made him look oddly defenseless, although Jenny knew he was a tough kid.

Unlike Summer, who hadn't had a tough sinew in her, Jenny thought. Summer had been as fragile as spun glass.

Ever since the night of the Game, Jenny's emotions had been like boats bumping at a thick canvas barrier—cut off from her but still nudging. But suddenly, at the sight of Cam, they burst through. Grief for Summer. Guilt. Tears filled her eyes.

What on earth could she say to him? "I'm sorry" was so inadequate it was pathetic.

Other kids were coming out of hiding at the sight of Audrey and Jenny, gathering around curiously. Jenny still couldn't speak. Audrey came to the rescue, improvising.

"So what are you playing?"

"Lambs and monsters," Cam said. "I'm the monster."

"Oh. So how do you play it?"

Kiah spoke up. "If you're a lamb you hide, and then the monster comes looking for you. And if he tags you, then you're captured and you have to go back to the monster lair. And you have to stay there until another lamb comes and lets you out—"

"Or until the monster eats you," Cam put in harshly.

Kiah's eyes flashed. "But he *can't* eat you until he's got all the lambs there. Ev-er-y sin-gle one."

Cops and robbers, Jenny thought. With only one cop and lots of robbers. The new name seemed a little savage, though, and so did the look in Cam-the-monster's eyes. God, I wonder what it must be like for him at home, she thought.

"Cam," she said. His hard blue eyes fixed on her. "Cam, did your parents tell you what we said happened to Summer?"

He nodded tightly.

"Well—" Jenny had a feeling that Aba might not approve of what she was going to do next. But all these kids knew Cam, they cared. Jenny felt more of a connection here than she had anywhere else.

"Well—I know it sounds crazy. I know your mom and dad don't believe it. But, Cam, it was the *truth*. We didn't hurt Summer, and we didn't mean to let anybody else hurt her. You just don't know how sorry—" The tears spilled suddenly, embarrassingly. Cam looked away and Jenny tried to get a grip on herself.

"And what we're doing now is trying to stop the person who hurt her from hurting anybody else," she whispered, feeling stupidly like somebody on TV— "America's Most Wanted."

Joey had joined the group and was flushed to his yellow hair roots with the humiliation of having a teenage sister bawling on the sidewalk. But Cam's tight look eased slightly.

"You mean all that stuff kids are saying about you guys looking for a cardboard house is true?"

"Are they saying that? Good." It's working, Jenny thought. The junior grapevine. There was something heartening in these kids' expressions. They weren't closed off like adults, but open, interested, speculative. "Listen," she said. "We're still looking for that house, and now we're looking for something else. A girl who was friends with P.C. Serrani." For the hundredth time that day she described the Crying Girl.

The kids listened.

"We really, really want to talk to her," Jenny said.

Then she explained why. Why they needed the girl and why they needed the house. She explained, more or less, about Julian. A watered-down version, but the truth.

When she finished, she let out a long breath—and saw something like determination coalescing in the steady young gazes. They'd weighed her claims, and they were willing to give her the benefit of the doubt. Even Joey, who'd been running away from her for the last two weeks, looked halfway convinced.

"We'll look for the girl tomorrow," he said briefly. "We'll talk to kids who've got, like, brothers or sisters in junior high. Because they might know her."

"Exactly!" Jenny said, pleased. She spared him the humiliation of being kissed by his sister in public. "Just be careful. If you see the paper house, *do not* touch it."

The last traces of doubt were wiped from the young faces, and there were grim nods. Her urgency had gotten through. She felt as if she'd recruited a team of small private detectives.

"Thanks," she said, and, feeling it was time for a judicious retreat, she gestured Audrey toward the next house.

"One more game," somebody behind her said, and somebody else said, "But who's going to be It?"

"Cam, unless he can guess who puts the eye in," Kiah's sweet voice fluted. On the doorstep Jenny glanced toward the street.

Cam was turned around, undergoing some elaborate ritual for picking the next It. "I draw a snake upon your back," Kiah chanted, tracing a wiggly shape. "Who will put in the eye?"

Somebody lunged forward and poked Cam between the shoulder blades. "Courtney!" Cam shouted.

"Wrong! You're the monster again!"

The door opened to Audrey's knocking. "Yes?"

Jenny tried to tear her attention from the game. Something about it . . . and about that snake thing . . . were all children's games that gruesome? And their stories? *The better to eat you with, my dear.* . . .

Maybe kids know something adults don't know, Jenny thought, chilled, as a lady asked them into the house.

When they came out, the sky was periwinkle blue and losing its color to the east. The light was fading. The street was empty.

Good, Jenny thought, glad that Joey was on his way home—maybe even home by now.

"Want to finish this block?" Audrey said, surprising her.

"I—sure. Why not?"

They worked their way down one side of the street and up the other. Jenny could feel herself getting more and more perfunctory at each house. The sky was now midnight blue and the light had gone. She didn't know why, but she was starting to feel anxious.

"Let's stop here," she said when there were still three more houses to go. "I think we should be getting back now."

The midnight blue slowly turned to black. The streetlights seemed far apart, and Jenny was reminded suddenly of the little islands of light in Zach's nightmare. A nightmare where a hunter had chased them through endless darkness.

"Hey, wait up!" Audrey protested.

Jenny grabbed her arm. "No, you hurry up. Come on, Audrey, we have to get back to the car."

"What do you mean? What's wrong with you?

"I don't know. We just have to get back!" A primitive warning was going off in Jenny's brain. A warning from the time when girls took skin bags to get water, she thought wildly, remembering something she'd sensed with Julian. A time when panthers walked in the darkness outside mud huts. When darkness was the greatest danger of all.

"Jenny, this is just so totally unlike you! If there was anything to be scared about, *I'd* be scared of it," Audrey said, resisting as Jenny dragged her along. "You're the one who always used to go off into the bad parts of town—"

"Yes, and look where it got me!" Jenny said. Her heart was pounding, her breath coming fast. "Come on!"

"—and I hate to tell you, but I *can't* run in these shoes. They've been killing me for hours now."

The flickering streetlight showed Audrey's tight Italian pumps. "Oh, Audrey, why didn't you say something?" Jenny said in dismay. Something made her jerk her head around, looking behind her. Something rustled in the oleanders.

Where everyone else only sees a wind in the grass, or a shadow . . .

"Audrey, take your shoes off. Now!"

"I can't run barefoot—"

"Audrey, there is something behind us. We have to get out of here, fast. Now, *come on!"* She was pulling Audrey again almost before Audrey had gotten the pumps off. Walking as fast as she could without running. If you run, they chase you, she thought wildly. But she wanted to run.

Because there *was* something back there. She could hear the tiny sounds. It was tracking them, behind the hedge of overgrown bushes on her right. She could feel it watching them.

Maybe it's Cam or one of the other kids, she thought, but she knew it wasn't. Whatever it was, she knew in her heart that it wanted to hurt them.

It was moving quickly, lightly, keeping pace with them maybe twenty feet back. "Audrey, hurry. . . ."

Instead, Audrey stopped dead. Jenny could just make out her look of fear as she stood, listening.

"Oh, God, there *is* something!"

The rustling was closer.

We should have run for a house, Jenny realized. Her one thought had been to get to the car. But now they had passed the last houses before the school grounds, and Audrey's car was too far ahead. They weren't going to make it.

"Come on!" Don't run don't run don't run, the hammering inside Jenny said. But her feet, clammy

in their summery mesh loafers, wanted to pound
down the sidewalk.

It was gaining on them.

It can't be a person—a person would show above
those hedges, Jenny thought, casting a look behind
her. Suddenly Jenny's brain showed her a terrible
picture: little Nori scurrying along spiderlike behind
the bushes, her face contorted in a grimace.

Don't run don't run don't run . . .

The car was ahead, looking black instead of red in
the darkness beyond a streetlight. Jenny seemed to
hear eerily rapid breath behind her.

Dontrundontrundontrundontrun . . .

"Get the keys," she gasped. "Get the *keys,*
Audrey—"

Here was the car. But the rustling was right beside
Jenny now, just on the other side of the hedge. It was
going to come *through* the hedge, she thought. Right
through the hedge and grab her. . . .

Audrey was fumbling in her purse. She'd dropped
her shoes. Jenny grabbed the car door handle.

"Audrey!" she cried, rattling it.

Audrey flung the contents of her purse on the
sidewalk. She scattered the pile with a desperate
hand, seized the keys.

"Audrey! Get it open!" Jenny watched in agony as
Audrey ran to the driver's side of the car, leaving the
contents of her purse scattered.

But it was too late. There was a crashing in the
hedge directly behind Jenny.

At the same moment a dark shape reared up from
the shadows on the sidewalk in front of her.

5

Jenny screamed.

Or got out half a scream anyway. The rest was cut off as something knocked her to the ground. It was the dark figure in front of her, and it was shouting something.

"Jenny, get down!"

Her brain only made sense of the words after she *was* down. There was a dull crashing and a thudding-and-rushing that might have been the blood in her ears. Then the crashing stopped.

"Wait, stay down until I see if it's gone," Tom's voice said. Jenny got up anyway, looking at him in amazement. What are you doing here? she thought. But what she said was "Did you see it?"

"No, I was looking at you. I *heard* it and then I—"

"—knocked me down," Jenny said. "Did you see it, Audrey?"

"Me? I was trying to get my door open, and then I

was trying to get *your* door open. I heard it go by, but when I looked it was gone."

"I don't think it went *by*," Tom said. "I think it went *over*—it ran over the hood of your car."

"It couldn't have," said Jenny. "A person wouldn't—" She stopped. Once again a horrible image of Nori, scampering spiderlike, entered her mind.

"I don't think it was a person," Tom began in a low voice. "I think—"

"Look!" Audrey said. "Down there past that streetlight—some kind of animal—" Her voice was high with fear.

"Turn on your headlights," Tom said.

A wedge of white light pierced the darkness. The animal was caught squarely in the beams, eyes reflecting green.

It was a dog.

Some sort of Lab mix, Jenny guessed. Black enough to blend into the night—or the hedges. It stared at them curiously, then its tail gave a quick, uncertain wag.

Rustlings in the bushes, Jenny thought. That tail wagging! And the quick, panting breath.

"Dog breath," she gasped aloud, almost hysterically. After the tension, the relief was acutely painful.

Audrey leaned her auburn head against the steering wheel.

"And for that I lost my shoes?" she demanded, sitting up and glaring at Jenny, who was hiccuping weakly.

"We'll go back and get them. I'm sorry. Honestly. But I'm glad *you're* here, anyway," Jenny said to Tom.

He was looking at the dog. "I don't think—" he began again. Then he shook his head and turned to her. "I didn't mean to hurt you."

"Didn't you?" Jenny said, not meaning the knocking-down. She looked up into his face.

He ducked away to help Audrey pick up her scattered belongings from the sidewalk. They could only find one shoe.

"Oh, leave it," Audrey said in disgust. "I don't care anymore. I only want to get home and soak for about an hour."

"You go on. Tom can take me home," Jenny said. Tom looked at her, seeming startled. "You do have your car, don't you? Or did you walk?"

"My car's down the street. But—"

"Then you can take me," Jenny said flatly. Audrey raised her eyebrows, then got in her car and drove away with a "Ciao" settling the matter.

Tom and Jenny walked slowly to Tom's RX-7. Once inside, though, Tom didn't start the engine. They just sat.

"Well, you've made yourself pretty scarce today," Jenny said. "While the rest of us were working." That hadn't come out right. She was upset, that was the problem.

Tom was fiddling with the radio, getting static. "I'm sorry, Jenny," he said. "I had things to do."

Where was his smile—that rakish, conspiratorial, sideways grin? He was treating her politely, like *anybody*.

Worse, he was calling her Jenny. When he was happy, he called her Thorny or some other silly name.

"Tom, what the *hell* is going on?"

46

"Nothing."

"What are you talking about, *nothing?* Tom, look at me! You've been avoiding me all day. What am I supposed to think? What's *happening?*"

Tom just shook his head slightly.

"You really have been avoiding me. On purpose." Jenny hadn't quite believed it herself until she put it into words. "Not just today, either. It's been ever since—" She stopped. "Tom. It's not—it hasn't got anything to do with—" She couldn't make herself say it; it was too ridiculous. But what other explanation was there?

"It hasn't got anything to do with what happened in the Game, has it? With—*him?*"

She could tell from the silence that she was right.

"Are you crazy?" Jenny said in a sort of quiet explosion.

"Let's just not talk about it."

"Let's just not talk about it?" Somewhere inside Jenny hysteria was building up, ready to be released.

"Look, I know the score. Maybe better than you do." In the faint light from the instrument panel, she could see that his mouth was grim.

Jenny got hold of herself and said carefully, "Tom, I am your girlfriend. I love you. We've always been together. And now suddenly you've changed completely, and you're acting like—like—"

"I'm not the one who's changed," he said. Then, turning fully toward her, he said, "Can you look at me and tell me you don't think about him?"

Jenny was speechless.

"Can you honestly tell me that? That you don't think about him, *ever?*"

"Only to be scared of him," Jenny whispered, her

throat dry. She had a terrible feeling, as if earthquakes and tidal waves were ahead of her.

"I saw you with him—I saw you looking at each other."

Oh, *God,* Jenny thought. Her mind was filled with panicked images. Julian's fingers in her hair, light as the soft pat of a cat's paw. Julian tilting her face up, Jenny flowing toward him. Julian supporting her weight, kissing the back of her neck. . . .

But Tom hadn't seen all that. He had only seen her and Julian together at the end, when Jenny's thoughts had been on getting her friends out of the paper house.

"I was trying to save us all," she said, safely on high moral ground. "You know that."

"And that means you didn't feel anything at all for him?"

Lie, Jenny thought. There was no reason she should have to lie. She *didn't* feel anything for Julian. But she was so confused—so frightened and confused—she didn't know what was going on anymore. *"No,"* she said.

"I know you, Jenny—I know when something gets to you. I saw you—respond to him. He brings out another side to you, makes you different."

"Tom—"

"And I saw what he can do, everything he can do. He's superhuman. How can I compete with that?"

And there, Jenny thought, clarity returning, was the problem. If Tom Locke the Flawless had a flaw, this was it. He was used to always winning, and winning easily. Tom didn't *do* anything he couldn't do right the first time. He wouldn't try if he thought he was going to fail.

"Besides, you don't need me anymore."

Oh. So that was what he thought.

Jenny shut her eyes.

"You're wrong," she whispered. "I needed you all day today. And you weren't there. . . ."

"Hey—oh, Jenny, don't cry. Hey, Jen." His voice had changed. He put a hand on her shoulder, then an arm around her. He did it awkwardly, as if it were the first time.

Jenny couldn't stop the tears.

"Don't cry. I didn't mean to make you cry." He leaned over to grip her other shoulder with his other hand.

Jenny opened wet eyes.

He was looking into her face, and he was so close. The grim expression was gone, and in its place was concern—and love. Anguished love. In that instant Jenny saw beneath the smooth, polished exterior of Tom Locke's defenses.

"Tommy . . ." she whispered, and her hand found his, their fingers locking together.

Then one or the other of them made a movement —Jenny never could remember which—and she was in his arms. They were holding on to each other desperately.

Relief flooded Jenny, and she gave a little sob. It felt so good to have Tom holding her again. In a moment he would kiss her, and everything would be all right.

But then—something happened. The RX-7's interior was small, like an airplane cockpit, and the center console curved out. Tom pulled back a bit in order to kiss her, and his hand or elbow knocked into the radio buttons. It must have, because suddenly music spilled into the car.

It was a song Jenny's mother sometimes played, an oldie by Dan Fogelberg. She had never really noticed the words before, but now they rang out clearly through the car.

"*. . . Like the songs that the darkness composes to worship the light. . . .*"

Jenny recoiled, heart jolting.

God, who had thought of that? Who had ever thought of that? What did some seventies songwriter know about darkness worshiping light?

She was staring at the radio, transfixed. Out of the corner of her eye she saw Tom staring at *her*.

Jenny reached out and jabbed at the radio, and the car was plunged into silence.

She had to say something—but her mind was blank. All she could hear was the echo of Julian's voice saying, *"I want her for . . . light to my darkness. You'll see—Tommy."*

The silence became terrible.

"I'd better get you home," Tom said in a voice as empty and polite as he had started with. "It's late."

"It was just a song," Jenny burst out, but she knew the song wasn't the problem. The problem was her reaction.

"You've changed, Jenny."

"I'm so tired of hearing that!" Jenny got her breath and added, "If I've changed so much, maybe you don't want me anymore. Maybe we should break up."

She had said it to shock. Stunned, she realized he wasn't going to contradict her.

"Better get you home," he said again.

Jenny desperately wanted to take the words back, but it was too late. It was too late for anything, and her pride wouldn't let her cry or speak. She sat frozen as they drove to her house. Tom walked her in.

Jenny's mother was standing on the threshold of the living room.

"And just where have you been?" she demanded. She had dark golden hair and a quick temper.

"It's my fault, Mrs. Thornton," Tom said.

"It is *not* his fault. I'm responsible for myself," Jenny said.

"As long as you're home," Mrs. Thornton said, with a sigh. Her temper, like Jenny's, flared quickly and died more quickly. "Are you hungry? Have you had dinner, Tom?"

Tom shook his dark head. "I'd better be getting home," he said, avoiding Jenny's eyes.

"Yes, you had," Mr. Thornton said softly but pointedly from his armchair. Jenny's father was a small man, but he had a sardonic eye that could kill from across the room. "I'm sure *your* parents are expecting you. And next time, be back before dark."

As the door closed behind him, Jenny said with reckless energy, "There probably won't be a next time."

Her mother was startled. "Jenny?"

Jenny turned toward the kitchen, but not before she saw her parents exchange glances. Her father shook his head, then went back to *Time* magazine.

Her mother followed her into the kitchen.

"Dear one—you *can't* be upset because we want you home early. We're just trying to keep you and Joey safe."

51

"It isn't that." Jenny was struggling with tears. "It's just—I think Tom and I are going to break up."

Her mother stared. "Oh, sweetheart!"

"Yes. And I just don't know—oh, Mom, everything's changing!" Abruptly Jenny threw herself into her mother's arms.

"Things do change, sweetheart. You're at the age when everything starts happening. I know how scary it can be, and I'm sorry about Tom—"

Jenny shook her head mutely. She and her mom had talked about growing up before. Jenny had always felt secretly a little smug at how well she was handling it all. She'd had it all planned out: high school with Tom, and then college with Tom, and then, in some comfortably fuzzy future, marriage to Tom, and an interesting career, and a world tour. After the tour, babies. Boy and girl, like that.

She'd already conquered growing up: she knew exactly what it was going to be like.

Not anymore. Her cozy future was crumbling around her.

She drew away from her mother.

"Jenny . . . Jenny, there isn't anything you're not telling us—say, about Zach? Because Aunt Lily is really worried. She says he's been acting so different. . . . He even seems to have lost interest in his photography. . . ."

Jenny could feel herself stiffen. "What kind of anything?" she said.

"Of course, we know Zach didn't—didn't hurt Summer in any way. But he wasn't the one who made up this story, was he? And you all believed it because you care about him." It was phrased as a theory, and Jenny was horrified.

"No," she said. "First of all, nobody made up the story." Although Mrs. Thornton continued to face her, Jenny noticed that her mother's golden-brown eyes went shades darker at that, and seemed to wall over. It was how all the parents looked when the kids talked about the reality of what had happened that night. They were listening, but they weren't listening. They believed you because you were their kid, but they *couldn't* believe you. So they ended up staring at you like polite zombies and making excuses behind their eyes.

"Nobody made the story up," Jenny repeated tiredly, already defeated. "Look—I'm really not hungry."

She escaped to the family room, where Joey was playing a video game—but it wasn't escape. The phone rang.

She reached for it automatically. "Hello?"

Shhshhshhshhshhshhshhshhshhshhshhshh.

Chills swept over Jenny.

The white noise went on, but over it there was a whispering. "A . . . ishhshhshhht . . ."

"Joey, turn the TV down!"

The breathy whisper came again, and Jenny heard the psychic's voice in her mind. *Vanished . . .*

"Van-ishhshhshhhed," the voice whispered.

Jenny clutched the phone, straining to hear. "Who is this?" She was suddenly angry rather than afraid. She had visions of the frosted-blond psychic on the other end. But the voice seemed like a man's, and it had a distorted quality to it that went beyond foreign. The word *sounded* like *vanished,* but . . .

The phone clicked, then there was a dial tone.

"What's wrong?" her mother said, coming in. "Did someone call?"

"Didn't you hear it ring?"

"I can't hear anything over that TV. Jenny, what is it? You're so pale."

"Nothing." She didn't want to talk about it with her mother. She couldn't stand any more questions —or any more weird stuff—or any more *anything*.

"I'm really tired," she said and headed for the back of the house before her mother could stop her.

In the privacy of her own room, she flopped on the bed. It was a pleasant room, and normally its familiarity would have comforted her. Michael always said it looked like a garden because of the Ralph Lauren comforter in rose and poppy and gold and dusty blue, and the baskets on the dresser twined with silk flowers. On the windowsill were pots of petunias and alyssum.

Just now it made Jenny feel—*alien*. As if she didn't belong to its familiarity any longer.

She lay listening to the house. She heard the distant sounds of the family room TV cut short, and presently heard splashing noises in the bathroom. Joey going to bed. Voices in the hall, and a door shutting. Her parents going to bed. After that, everything was quiet.

Jenny lay there a long time. She couldn't relax for sleep; she had to do something to express the strangeness she felt inside. She wanted—she wanted—

She wanted to do something ritual and—well, *purifying*. By herself.

Then she had it. She went to the door and cautiously turned the knob. She stepped into the darkened hallway, listening. Silence. Everyone was asleep; the house had that hushed middle-of-the-night feeling.

Quietly Jenny opened the linen closet and fished out a towel. Still careful not to make the slightest sound, she unlocked the family room sliding glass door and eased it open.

A three-quarter moon was rising over the foothills. Jenny glanced toward her parents' room, but their venetian blinds were dark, and a row of tall oleander bushes blocked their view of the pool. No one would see her.

She made her way stealthily to a block-wall alcove, where she turned a switch. The pool light went on.

Magic. It transformed a dark ominous void into a fluorescent blue-green jewel.

Jenny sighed.

Keeping well behind the screening row of bushes, she stripped her clothes off. Then she knelt by the lip of the pool, sat on it, easing her legs into the water. She could feel the porous concrete deck on the backs of her thighs and the cool water on her calves. She looked at her feet, pale green and magnified in the glowing water. With a careful twist and a slide, she dropped in.

A slight shock of coolness. Jenny boosted off the side of the pool with her feet and floated on her back, spreading her arms. The smell of chlorine filled her nostrils.

The moon was pure silver in the sky and very far away. Right now Jenny felt as distant from ordinary emotions.

So what do you do, she thought, floating, when you've sold your soul to the devil?

That was about the size of it. She had let Julian put

his ring on her finger. A gold ring with an inscription on the inside: *All I refuse and thee I chuse.*

Magical words, inscribed on the *inside* of the ring so they would rest against her skin and bind her to the promise.

When they'd gotten back from the Shadow World, Jenny had put the ring in the white box, the one with the paper house, the one P.C. and Slug had stolen. Now she wished she had it back. She should have had it melted down or hammered flat.

The water slipped pleasantly between her fingertips. It cradled her whole body, touching all her skin. It was a very—sensual—feeling, to be embraced like this, to stroke out in any direction and feel the coolness flow past you.

Jenny—felt things—more these days.

She'd discovered it that first week after getting back. She'd realized, to her bewilderment and somewhat to her horror, that she found things more beautiful than before. The night air was more fragrant than it used to be, her cat's fur was smoother. She noticed little things—tiny, delicate details she had never seen before.

Something about her time with Julian had—opened her to things. To their sensuality, their *immediacy*. Maybe that was what people were noticing when they said she had changed.

Or maybe she'd always been different. Because she'd been chosen. Julian had chosen her, had fallen in love with her, had begun to watch her, when she was five years old.

Because when she was five she had opened a secret closet in her grandfather's basement, a closet carved with the symbol Nauthiz, a rune of restraint.

56

It had been a natural thing to do. Let a kid alone in a cellar where a bookcase has been moved to expose a secret door, and what would anyone expect? What would be the harm?

It depended. If your grandfather was like any grandfather, a sweet old guy who liked gardening and golf, no harm. But if your grandfather was a dabbler in the black arts, it might be another story. And if your grandfather had actually succeeded in his ambition to call up spirits from another world, to trap them . . . and if the door you opened was the one that held them in . . .

The consequences had been unimaginable.

Jenny had opened that door and seen a whirling, seething mixture of ice and shadows. And in the shadows—eyes.

Dark eyes, watching eyes, sardonic, cruel, amused eyes. Ancient eyes. The eyes of the Others, the Shadow Men.

They were called different names in different ages, but always their essential nature came through. They were the ones who watched from the shadows. Who sometimes took people to—their own place.

The thing Jenny remembered most about the eyes was that they were hungry. Evil, powerful, and *ravenous.*

"They'd love to get a tooth in you," Julian had told Dee. *"All my elders, those ancient, bone-sucking, lip-licking wraiths."*

Suddenly the water seemed more cold than cool. Jenny swam over to the steps and got out, shivering.

In her room she rubbed herself dry until she stopped shivering. Then she put on a T-shirt and crawled into bed. But the vision of glowing eyes haunted her until she fell asleep from sheer exhaustion.

She woke up very suddenly when the phone rang.

The alarm, she thought, confused, and reached for the clock by her bedside. But the ringing went on.

Her window was dark. The clock in her hand showed a glowing red 3:35 A.M.

The ringing went on, frighteningly loud, like a siren.

Her parents would pick it up any minute now. But they didn't. Jenny waited. The ringing went on.

They *had* to pick it up. Not even Joey slept that soundly. Each burst of noise was like white lightning in the dark and silent house.

Chills ran over Jenny's skin.

She found that she had been counting unconsciously. Nine rings. Ten. Eleven. Twelve. Shattering the stillness.

Maybe it was Dee, maybe she and Michael had found out something important and for some reason hadn't been able to call until now.

Heart pounding, Jenny picked up the receiver.

"A isht," a voice whispered.

Jenny froze.

"A . . . isht . . ."

The formless electronic noise blurred the word. Jenny could only make out the vowel sounds and the soft shush at the end. *A* as in *amble*, then *shht*. It didn't sound exactly like *vanished* anymore.

She wanted to speak, but she couldn't. She could only clutch the phone and listen.

"A isht . . ."

Damaged? No, that was even farther off. A-isht. Am-ish. Amished.

Oh my *God*. Oh God oh God oh God . . .

Sheer black terror swept through her, and every hair on her body erected. She felt her eyes go wide and tears spring to them. In that instant she heard, really heard what the voice was saying. She *knew*.

Not *vanished*. It sounded like *vanished,* but it wasn't. It was something much worse. The whispery, distorted voice with the odd cadence was saying *famished*.

Famished.

Jenny threw the phone as hard as she could across the room. She was on her feet, her skin crawling, body washed with adrenaline. *Famished. Famished.* The eyes in the closet. The Shadow Men.

Those evil, *ravenous* eyes . . .

The better to *eat* you with, my dear.

6

It was that psychic," Dee said promptly. "She looked like a case of peroxide on the brain to me."

"No," said Michael. "You know what it really is?" Jenny thought he was going to make a joke, but for once he was serious. "It's battle fatigue. We've all got it. We're stressed to the max, and we're seeing—and hearing—things that aren't there."

It was the next day. They were all sitting on the grassy knoll—all but Tom, of course. Jenny was surprised that Zach had shown up. After what she'd said to him at lunch yesterday, she'd have thought he'd have withdrawn from them all. But he was in his place, long legs folded under him, ashy-blond head bent over his lunch.

Jenny herself had no appetite. "The calls weren't hallucinations," she said. It was all she could do to keep her voice steady. "Okay, the last one might have been a dream—I woke up my parents screaming, and they said *they* didn't hear the phone ring. But the other times—I was walking around, Michael. I was awake."

"No, no, I'm not saying the phone calls aren't real. I'm saying the phone rang, and maybe somebody even whispered something at you—or maybe it was just static—but you imagined what it was saying. You put your own interpretation on the sounds. You didn't hear *vanished* until the psychic said *vanished,* right?"

"Yes," Jenny said slowly. In the bright May sunshine, the terror of last night seemed less real. "But—it wasn't like imagining it. I *heard* the sounds the first time when the phone rang at school, and in the end they came clear. And the word made sense. Not *vanished,* but *famished*—it fit in with those eyes."

"But that's just why you imagined it." Michael was waving a box of Cracker Jack, warming to his subject. "Maybe *imagined* isn't the right word. See, your brain is like a modeling system. It takes the input it gets from your senses and makes the most reasonable model it can from it. But when you're really stressed, it can take that input—like somebody whispering nonsense on the phone—and make the *wrong* model out of it. Your brain hears something that isn't there. It seems real because it *is* real—to your brain."

Dee was frowning, clearly not liking the idea of not relying on her brain. "Yes, but it *isn't* real."

"It's as real as any of the other models your brain makes all day. Like—last night I was doing homework in my living room, and my brain made a model of a coffee table. That's what it thought of the images my eyes were showing it. It took *wood* and *rectangu-*

lar and matched that with *coffee table,* and I recognized it. But if I was really stressed, I might see *wood* and *rectangular,* and my brain might make a model of a coffin. Especially if I'd been asleep or if I was already thinking about coffins. See?"

Jenny did, sort of.

"But the coffin still wouldn't be *real,*" Dee argued.

"But how could I tell?

"Easy. You could touch it—"

"Touching's just another sense. It could be fooled, too. No, if a model's good enough, there would be *no way* to tell it wasn't real," Michael said.

It made sense, Jenny thought. It was like the dog yesterday evening. She'd been jumping at shadows because she was so frightened.

She sat back on the grassy knoll and let out a deep breath. The knot in her stomach had eased slightly— and now she could worry about other things.

Like Tom. As long as he wasn't there, things wouldn't be right.

The others were talking around her.

"—we covered about half the streets yesterday," Dee was saying, "but we didn't find anything—"

"I found blisters," Michael put in.

"And if I keep missing my kung fu classes I'm not going to *live* through the next competition," Dee finished.

"You think you've got problems? *I* found scratches all over the hood of the Spider this morning," Audrey said. "Daddy's going to kill me when he sees it." She told the story of the dog that had followed them. Michael spilled his Cracker Jack in triumph.

"You see? More modeling," he said. But Audrey

pushed down her designer sunglasses with one finger to stare over them.

"Jenny?" she said. "What's wrong?"

They were all looking at her.

Jenny could feel her lips tremble slightly, but she tried to sound off-hand. "It's just—Tom and I had a fight. And we sort of . . ." She shrugged. "Well, I don't know if we're together anymore or not."

They all stared as if she'd said the world was ending in a few minutes.

Then Michael whistled and ran his hands through his hair, rumpling it even more wildly. Dee, who normally scorned anything to do with romance, put a slender, night-dark hand on Jenny's arm. Audrey's eyebrows were hiked up into her spiky copper bangs. Zach shook his head, a distant flicker of ice in his winter-gray eyes.

Audrey was the first to recover. "Don't worry, *chéri,*" she said, taking the sunglasses off and snapping them into a case briskly. "It's not permanent. Tom just needs some stirring up. Guys need to be reminded of their place every so often," she added with a severe glance at Michael, who spluttered.

"No. It wasn't a regular fight. It was about *him*—Julian. He thinks I belong to Julian or something, like one of those horrible old movies. Bride of the Devil. He thinks he's lost me already, so why compete?" She told them about it as best she could.

Audrey listened, her narrowed eyes turned in the direction of the English building. Suddenly her lips curved in a catlike smile. "Clearly, drastic measures are called for. And I have an idea," she said.

"What idea?"

Audrey nodded toward the building. Taped to the brick was a large poster reading: Come to the Midnight Masquerade. *"Voilà."*

"Voilà?" Jenny said blankly.

"The prom. Brian Dettlinger. Yesterday. Remember?"

"Yes, but—"

"You said Tom thinks he can't compete with a demon lover. But maybe if he sees he's got *human* competition, he'll get a little more motivated."

Jenny stared at her. It was crazy—and it just might work. "But I told Brian no. He'll have another date by now."

"I don't *think* so," Audrey hummed. "I got the dirt from Amy Cheng yesterday in algebra. Brian dumped Karen Lalonde to ask you."

Jenny blinked. Karen Lalonde was the head cheerleader. Beautiful. Brilliant. Magnetic. "He dumped her—for me?"

"They've been on the rocks for a while. Karen's been seeing Davoud Changizi on the side. But Brian put up with it until now."

"But—"

"Listen to me, Jenny. After what Tom's done, who can blame you for looking elsewhere? Besides, you'll probably have a great time—it's *Brian Dettlinger*, for heaven's sake. I tell you what; I'll even go with you. I know I can rustle up a date somewhere."

Michael yowled in protest. *"What?"*

"Now, Michael, don't fuss. I'm not going for *fun;* it's like Mother's charities—all for a good cause. Don't you want Jenny and Tom to get back together?"

Michael was spluttering again. But Dee was grinning her wildest grin. "Go on, Sunshine," she said. "Make it happen."

Zach crumpled his lunch sack, looking bored with the whole situation.

"Now, come on," Audrey said. "If we hurry, we should be able to find him before the bell rings. *Allez!* This will be easy."

It was. Brian looked surprised when Jenny walked up—but a light went on in his eyes. Seeing that light, Jenny suddenly knew that he hadn't found another date.

It was odd having a senior look at her like that. Suddenly Jenny wondered again if it was fair to do this. She thought about Aba's maxims, the ones Dee's grandmother had taped to the mirror in her bathroom. A simple hand-lettered sign saying:

> Do no harm.
> Help when you can.
> Return good for evil.

In the Game Jenny had understood how necessary those maxims were if the world wasn't going to become the kind of place Julian said it was. She'd resolved to live by them. This didn't seem to fit.

But it was too late now. Audrey was talking with Brian, teasing him, letting him know what Jenny was there for. It was all being arranged.

"I'll pick you up at seven," Brian was saying, and there was something like excitement in his face. He was looking at her eyes, at her hair across her shoulders. She could hardly tell him she'd changed her mind now.

"Fine," Jenny said weakly and let Audrey lead her away.

What have I done? I don't even have a dress—

The bell rang.

Jenny, Michael, and Audrey had algebra together, then Jenny went to computer applications. That was where Michael's theory about brain modeling was put to the test.

It started with the keyboard fouling up. Jenny's partner was absent, so she was alone at her computer, a glacier-slow IBM clone.

She was typing in her name when the *J* key stuck. She'd barely touched it with her right index finger, but the *J*s went on and on across the line. They got to the right margin and went on, got to the edge of the screen and went on.

The screen scanned right and the rest of Jenny's document moved jerkily to the left, disappearing. She stared in horror, her first thought that she'd broken the computer. Jenny loved computers, unlike Dee who hated technology, but she had to admit there was something a little *odd* about them, a little unnerving. As if *things* might happen unexpectedly there on screen. When she was a kid, after a day of playing with her dad's PC, Jenny had sometimes had dreams of bizarre scenes and impossible games appearing on the monitor. As if a computer wasn't just a machine but some kind of connection that could hook into the unknown.

Now her eyes widened as the *J*s went on. On and on and on. That wasn't right—that couldn't be. Where was word wrap? The letters should just fall down onto the next line.

They didn't. They kept going. A line of *J*s hitting the edge of the screen and then ebbing back as the screen scanned right, then surging to the edge again. Like a snake. Or something pulsing.

Jenny's little fingers were tingling; there was a crawling between her shoulder blades. This was *wrong*. She had a dreadful feeling of the physical distance the line of *J*s had traveled. It was as if she were out in space somewhere, far to the right of her original document—and going on farther. She was lost somewhere in virtual space, and she was terrified of what she might see there.

JJJJJJJJJJJJJJJJJJJJJJJJJJJJJJJJJJJJJJJJJJJJJJ

Jenny had been pressing Escape continuously since the key had stuck. Now she hit Enter to put in a hard return, to break the line. Nothing happened.

JJJJJJJJJJJJJJJJJJJJJJJJJJJJJJJJJJJJJJJJJJJJJJJ

Oh, God, what was out here? What were the *J*s heading for? Something miles to the side of her original document, something that just couldn't be there because there wasn't room for it. She was beyond any possible margins. It was like sailing over the edge of the world.

She scrambled in her mind for the screen rewrite code, hit that. Nothing. She stabbed at the Break key. Nothing. Then, teeth sunk in her lip, she pressed Control/Alt/Delete.

The combination should have rebooted the computer. It didn't. The *J*s sailed on.

The screen glowed a deep and beautiful blue. Jenny had never noticed before just how blue that screen really was. A color vivid beyond imagining.

The white *J*s surged on and on. Jenny had a physical sense of falling. She was out *too far.* . . .

She reached out and did something the computer teacher had threatened them with death for doing; she flipped the main switch of the computer off. Depriving it of electricity, killing it in the middle of a program. Crashing it deliberately.

Only it didn't crash.

The switch was off, the CPU light was off—but the *J*s kept on going, pulsing and surging.

Jenny's breath stopped. She stared in disbelief. Her hand went to the monitor and fumbled frantically with the monitor switch. It clicked under her fingers; the monitor light went off.

"What are you *doing?*" the girl to the left of her gasped.

The monitor still glowed blue. The *J*s sailed on.

Jenny yanked the keyboard out of the socket.

She had to stop this. Something was going terribly, unimaginably wrong, and she had to stop those *J*s before . . .

"Ms. Godfrey!" the girl to the left of her cried. "Ms. Godfrey, Jenny's—"

Jenny had just an instant to see what happened next. Even with the keyboard detached, the *J*s kept going—or at least she thought they did. It was hard to tell because everything happened so fast. There was a bright flash—the screen going blindingly white —and a blue afterimage printed on her retinas. Then the monitor went dark.

So did the lights in the room—and all the other computers.

"Now see what you did," the girl beside her hissed.

Jenny sat, scarcely breathing. Pulling out the keyboard cord couldn't have caused a blackout. Even crashing her computer shouldn't have done that. The room wasn't totally dark, but it was very dim; the windows were tinted to protect the equipment. Impressed on the dimness Jenny saw pinwheels and filaments of glowing blue.

Oh, please, she thought, holding herself as still as possible. She could feel her heart beating in her throat.

Then she heard—something—from underneath the computer tables.

Soft as a match strike, but audible. A moving sound, like a rope being dragged. Like something sliding across the floor.

Toward her.

Jenny twisted her head, trying to locate it. The teacher's voice seemed distant. The sliding sound was getting closer, she could hear it clearly now. Like a dry leaf blowing across pavement. Starting and stopping. Surging. Like the *J*s. Coming straight for her legs.

It was almost here. Almost was under her table. And she couldn't move; she was frozen.

She heard a hiss like static. Like white noise. Or—

Something brushed her leg.

Jenny screamed. Released from her paralysis all at once, she jumped to her feet, beating at her leg. The thing brushed her again, and she grabbed at it, throttling it, trying to kill it—

—and found herself holding the keyboard cord.

It must have fallen over the edge of the table when she yanked it out, and dangled there. Jenny was

69

holding on to its spiraling length so tightly that she could feel dents in her palms. This close she could see it clearly. Just a cord.

The lights went on. People were gathering around her, putting their hands on her, asking questions.

It's just your brain making models, she told herself desperately, ignoring everyone else. The computer malfunctioned and you freaked. You heard static when the power went off, and you freaked more and made it into a hiss. But it wasn't real. It was just models in your brain.

"I think you'd better go home for the day," Ms. Godfrey said. "You look as if you could use some rest."

"I've got it figured out now," she said to Michael that night. "It must have been something to do with the UPS—the uninterruptible power supply. That's a kind of battery that keeps the computers going when the power goes out."

"Oh, right," said Michael, who knew very little about computers but would never admit it.

"That's what kept the computer going, but then somehow I managed to blow the whole system," Jenny said. "That knocked the power out, and all the rest of it was in my mind."

"You must have looked pretty funny holding that cord," Michael said.

They talked about what had happened to him and the others that afternoon. He and Dee and Audrey had gone postering together and had covered most of the area between Ramona and Anchor streets. They hadn't found anything.

Jenny told him what she'd told Dee and Audrey

earlier. She was okay now. She'd slept all afternoon. Her mother had wanted to take her to the doctor, but Jenny had said no.

She was very proud of herself for realizing it had all been in her mind. She planned to stay calmer in the future.

"Well, that's good," Michael said. His voice sounded surprisingly weak for somebody whose theory had been confirmed. "Uh, Jenny—"

"What?"

"Oh, nothing. See you tomorrow. Take care of yourself."

"You, too," Jenny said, a little startled. "Bye."

Michael stared at the cordless phone he'd just clicked off. Then he glanced uneasily at his bedroom window. He wondered if he should have told Jenny —but Jenny had enough to worry about.

Besides, there was no reason to do anything to tarnish his own brilliant theory. It *was* just battle fatigue, and he was as subject to it as anyone else.

Stress. Tension. In his own case combined with a rather nervous temperament. Michael had always claimed to be an unashamed coward.

That would account for the feeling he'd had all day of being watched. And there was nothing really moving outside that window. It was a second-floor apartment, after all.

Audrey stretched in her Christian Dior nightgown and deposited herself more haphazardly across the peach satin sheets. Even after forty-five minutes in the Jacuzzi her feet hurt. She was sure she was getting calluses.

Worse, she couldn't shake the strange sensation she'd had ever since this afternoon. It was the feeling Audrey usually had when entering a room—of eyes on her. Only these eyes today hadn't been admiring. They had been watchful—and malicious. She'd felt as if something were following her.

Stalking her.

Probably just the remnants of yesterday's fright. There was nothing to worry about—she was safe at home. In bed.

Audrey stretched again and her mind wandered. Eyes . . . hmm. No eyes now. *C'est* okay. *Va bène.*

She slept.

And dreamed, pleasantly. She was a cat. Not a repulsive scroungy cat like Jenny's, but an elegant Abyssinian. She was curled up with another cat, getting a cat-bath.

Audrey smiled responsively, ducking her head, exposing the nape of her neck to the seductive feeling. The other cat's tongue was rough but nice. It must be a *big* cat, though, she thought, half-waking. Maybe a tiger. Maybe—

With a shriek Audrey bolted straight up in bed. She was awake—but she could swear the sensation had followed her out of the dream. She *had* felt a rough tongue licking her neck.

She clapped a hand to the back of her neck and felt the dampness there.

A strange, musky smell filled the room.

Audrey almost knocked the bedside lamp over getting it turned on. Then she stared around wildly, looking for the thing that had been in her bed.

7

Dee woke with a start. At least she thought she woke—but she couldn't move.

Someone was leaning over her.

The room was very dark. It shouldn't have been, because Dee liked to sleep with the window open, the curtains drawn back. Breathing fresh air, not the stale refrigerated stuff that came out of the air conditioner.

Tonight she must have forgotten to open the curtains. Dee couldn't tell because she couldn't move her head. She could only see what was directly above her—the figure.

It was a thick darkness against the thinner darkness of the room. It was a human shape, upside-down because it was leaning over from the headboard side.

Dee's heart was pounding like a trip-hammer. She could feel her lips draw back from her teeth savagely.

Then she realized something horrifying.

The headboard side—the figure was leaning over her from the headboard side. *But there was a wall there.* It was leaning out of the *wall.*

"Get away from me!"

Shouting broke the spell. She vaulted off the bed, landing in a tangle of sheets in the middle of her room. She kicked the sheets free and was at the light switch by the door in one movement.

Light filled the room, glowing off the ocher walls. There was no dark figure anywhere.

Tacked over the bed between an African mask and a length of embroidered cloth from Syria was a poster. A poster of Bruce Lee. It was just where the figure had been.

Dee approached it slowly, warily, ready for anything. She got close and looked at it. Just an ordinary poster. Bruce Lee's image stared out blandly over her head. There was something almost smug about his expression. . . .

Abruptly Dee reached out and ripped the poster off the wall, scattering pushpins. She crumpled it with both hands and threw it in the general direction of the wastebasket.

Then she sat back against the headboard, breathing hard.

Zach had been lying for hours, unable to get to sleep. Too many thoughts crowding his brain. Thoughts—and images.

Him and Jenny as kids. Playing Indians in the cherry orchard. Playing pirates in the creek. Always playing something, lost in some imaginary world. Because imaginary worlds were better than the real thing. Safer, Zach had always thought.

Zach breathed out hard. His eyes fluttered open—and he shouted.

Suspended in the air above him was the head of a twelve-point buck.

It was hanging inches from his nose, so close his dark-adjusted eyes could see it clearly. But he was paralyzed. He wanted to twist to the side, to get away from it, but his arms and legs wouldn't obey.

It was falling on him!

His whole body gave a terrible jerk and adrenaline burst through him. His arm flung up to ward the thing off. His eyes shut, anticipating the blow.

It never came. He dropped his arm, opened his eyes.

Empty air above him.

Zach struck out at it anyway. Only believing it was gone when his hand encountered no resistance.

He got up and turned on the lights. He didn't stay to look around the room, though. He went downstairs, to the den, flipping on the lights there.

On the wood-paneled wall where his father's trophies hung, the twelve-pointer rested in its usual place.

Zach looked into its liquid-dark glass eyes. His gaze traveled over the splendid antlers, the shockingly delicate muzzle, the glossy brown neck.

It was all real and solid. Too heavy to move, bolted to the wall.

Which means maybe I'm losing my mind. Imagination gone completely wild. That would be a laugh, wouldn't it, to get through the Game and then come home and lose my mind over nothing?

Ha ha.

The den was as still as a photograph around him.

He wasn't going to get any sleep tonight. Normally, he would have gone out to his darkroom in the garage and done some work. That was what he'd always done before when he couldn't sleep.

But that had been—before. Tonight he'd rather just stare at the ceiling. Nothing else was any use.

"Hypnopompic hallucination," Michael said to Dee the next morning. "That's when you think you've woken up, but your mind is still dreaming. The dark figure in your room is a classic example. They even have a name for it—the Old Hag Syndrome. Because some people think it's an old lady sitting on their chest, paralyzing them."

"Right," Dee said. "Well, that's what it must have been, then. Of course."

"Same with you, Zach," Michael said, turning to look at him. "Only yours was *hypnagogic* hallucination—you thought you weren't asleep yet, but your brain was in la-la land already."

Zach said nothing.

"What about me?" Audrey said. "I *was* asleep—but when I woke up, my dream was true." She touched polished fingernails to the back of her neck, just beneath the burnished copper French twist. "I was *wet.*"

"Sweat," Michael said succinctly.

"I don't sweat."

"Well, ladylike perspiration, then. It's been hot."

Jenny looked around at the group on the knoll. They all sounded so calm and rational. But Michael's grin was strained, and Zach was paler than ever. Dee's nervous energy was like an electrical field. Audrey's lips were pressed together.

In spite of the brave words, they were all on edge.

And where's Tom? Jenny thought. He should *be* here. No matter what he thinks of me, he should be here for the sake of the others. What's he doing?

"I heard there was a body found up in the Santa Ana foothills," Dee said. "A guy from this school."

"Gordon Wilson," Audrey said, wrinkling her nose. "You know—that senior with the cowboy boots. People say he runs over cats."

"Well, he's not going to run over any more. They think a mountain lion got him."

Tom had heard about the body yesterday afternoon. and his first irrational thought had been: *Zach? Michael?*

But they had both been safe. And Jenny was safe at school today—although maybe school wasn't so safe, either. Yesterday, she'd gotten herself sent home from computer applications after something —it was hard to figure out exactly what from the conflicting stories—had happened.

A brief thought crossed his mind that he might call her and ask—but Tom had already chosen his course. He couldn't change it now, and she probably wouldn't want him to. He'd *seen* her in the car, that look when the song came on. Scared, yes, but with something underneath the scaredness. She'd never looked like that at him.

It didn't matter. He'd protect her anyway. But yesterday, knowing she was home for good, he'd taken the afternoon off and gone to the police station. He'd used charm on a female detective and learned exactly where the body had been found.

Today he was skipping school completely. Teachers were going to start asking questions about that soon.

So what?

Tom found the dry creek bed. It wasn't too far from the famous Bell Canyon Trail, where a six-year-old had been attacked by a mountain lion. The air was scented with sage.

There was a crinkled yellow "crime scene" ribbon straggling along the creek bed and little flags of various colors planted in the ground. Tom scrambled down the slope and stood where tiny traces of a dark stain on the rocks still showed.

He looked around. One place on the opposite bank had seen a lot of activity. Cactus had been broken, pineapple weed uprooted. There were footprints in the dirt.

Tom followed the trail up to a slope covered with purple sage. Coastal live oak and spreading syca-mores cast an inviting shade nearby.

Tom studied the ground.

After a moment he began to walk, slowly, toward the trees. He skirted brush. He came to three old sycamores growing so closely that their branches were entwined.

The air was heavier here. It had a strange smell. Very faint, but disturbing. Feral.

Like a predator.

Sometimes there were huge patches of poison ivy under these old trees. Tom looked carefully, then stirred the brush underneath with his foot. The smell came stronger. Something heavy had lain here for quite some time.

He turned and retraced his steps slowly.

Then he saw it. On a dusty rock directly between the trees and the place where the creek bank was disturbed. A splatter of black like tar. A thick, viscous substance that looked as if it had bubbled at the edges.

Tom's breath hissed in, and he knelt, eyes narrowed.

There was no sign that any of it had been scraped off. Either the police hadn't seen it or they hadn't cared. It clearly wasn't the blood of anything on earth. It didn't look like anything important.

It was. It was very important. Tom took out a Swiss army knife and scraped some of the gunk up to examine it. It had an odd, musky smell, and spread very thin it was not black but red.

Then he sat back on his heels and shut his eyes, trying to maintain the control he was famous for.

By Thursday Jenny noticed that Zach had dark circles under his eyes and Dee was jumpier than ever. Michael's face was blotchy, and one of Audrey's nails actually looked bitten.

They were all falling apart.

Because of dreams. That was all they were. Nothing really happened at night, nothing hurt them. But the dreams were enough.

Friday they were scheduled to go postering, but Jenny had to stop by the YMCA first, a few blocks from the Center. And it was there that something really did happen at last.

Jenny had been waiting so long, searching for so long, that she ought to have been prepared. But when the time came, she found she wasn't prepared at all.

She was inside the Y, talking to Mrs. Birkenkamp, the swim coach. Jenny volunteered every Friday with the swim class for disabled kids. She loved it and hated to miss.

"But I have to," she said miserably. "And maybe next Friday, too. I should have told you before, but I forgot—"

"Jenny, it's okay. Are *you* okay?"

Jenny lifted her eyes to the clear blue ones which looked at her steadily. There was something so wise about them—Jenny had the sudden impulse to throw herself into the woman's arms and tell her everything.

Mrs. Birkenkamp had been Jenny's hero for years. She never gave up or lost faith. She'd taught a child without arms to swim. Maybe she would have an answer.

But what could Jenny say? Nothing that an adult would believe. Besides, it was up to Jenny to do things for herself now. She couldn't rely on Tom anymore; she had to stand on her own feet.

"I'll be fine," she said unsteadily. "Tell all the kids hello—"

That was when Cam came in.

Dee was behind him. She had been waiting outside in her jeep. "He came over from the Center. He won't talk to anybody but you," she said.

Cam said simply, "I found her."

Jenny gasped. She actually felt dizzy for an instant. Then she said, *"Where?"*

"I got her address." Cam thrust a hand into the pocket of his skin-tight jeans and pulled out a grimy slip of paper.

"Right," Jenny said. "Let's go."

"Wait," Mrs. Birkenkamp said. "Jenny, what's all this about—"

"It's all right, Mrs. Birkenkamp," Jenny said, whirling around and hugging the willowy coach. "Everything's going to be all right now." She really did feel that way.

Cam directed them to the house. "Her name's Angela Seecombe. Kimberly Hall's big sister Jolie knows a guy who knows her. This is the street."

Filbert Street. East of Ramona Street, where P.C. lived, just south of Landana. Audrey and Jenny had been there, distributing flyers.

But not inside this yellow two-story house with the paint-chipped black iron fence. Jenny couldn't remember why they hadn't been let in here, but they hadn't.

"You stay here," she said. "I've got to do this myself. But, Cam—thank you." She turned to look at him, this tough kid with dandelion-fluff hair whose life had changed because his sister had gone to a party.

He shrugged, but his eyes met hers, grateful for the acknowledgment. "I wanted to."

No one answered the door of the yellow house. Jenny leaned on the bell.

Still no answer. But faintly, from inside, came the sound of a TV set.

Jenny glanced at the driveway. No car there. Maybe no adults home. She waved to Dee and Cam to stay in the car, then went around the side of the house. She unlatched the creaking iron gate and waded through thigh-deep foxtails to the back porch.

81

She grasped the knob of the back door firmly. Then she cast a look heavenward, took a deep breath, and tried it.

It was unlocked. Jenny stepped inside and followed the sound of the TV into a small family room.

Sitting on a rust-colored couch was the Crying Girl.

She jumped up in astonishment at the sight of Jenny, spilling popcorn from a microwave bag onto the carpet. Her long dark hair swung over her shoulders. Her haunted eyes were wide, and her mouth was open.

"Don't be afraid," Jenny said. "I'm not going to hurt you. I told you before, I need to talk to you."

Hatred flashed through the girl's face.

"I don't want to talk to *you!*" She darted to the telephone. "I'm calling the police—you're trespassing."

"Go ahead and call them," Jenny said with a calm she didn't feel. "And I'll tell them that you know things you haven't told them about the morning P.C. disappeared. You saw P.C., didn't you? You know where he went." She was gambling. Angela had threatened to tell in the beginning; in the bathroom she'd said she could prove P.C. didn't kill Summer. But she *hadn't* told—which must mean she didn't want to. Jenny was gambling that Angela would rather tell her than the police.

The girl said nothing, her slim olive-tan hand resting on the phone limply.

"Angela." Jenny went to her as she had four days ago in the high school bathroom. She put her hands on the girl's shoulders, gently this time.

"You *did* see P.C., didn't you? And you saw what

he had with him. Angela, you've got to tell me. You don't understand how important it is. If you don't tell me, the thing that happened to P.C. could happen to other people."

The small bones under Jenny's hands lifted as Angela heaved in a shaky breath.

"I hate you. . . ."

"No, you don't. You want something to hate because you hurt so much. I understand that. But I'm not your enemy, and I'm not a soshe or a prep or any of those things. I'm just another girl like you, trying to cope, trying to stop something bad from happening. And I hurt, too."

Dark, pensive eyes studied her face. "Oh, yeah?"

"Yeah. Like hell. And if you don't believe it, you're not as smart as you look." Jenny's nose and eyes were stinging. "Listen, Summer Parker-Pearson was one of my best friends. I lost her. Now I've lost my boyfriend over this, too. I just don't want anything worse to happen—which it will, if you don't help me."

Angela's eyes dropped, but not before Jenny saw the shimmer of tears.

Jenny spoke softly. "If you know where P.C. went that morning, then you have to tell me now."

Angela shrugged off Jenny's hands and turned away. Her entire body was tense for a moment, then it slumped. "I won't tell you—but I'll show you," she said.

"Jenny? Are you in there?"

Dee's voice, from the back door. As Dee appeared, narrow-eyed and moving like a jaguar, Jenny reached out quickly to Angela. "It's okay. She's my friend. You can show us both."

The girl hesitated, then nodded, giving in.

To Jenny's surprise, she didn't head for the front door, but led them out back. Cam followed them through the foxtails. The backyard sloped down to dense brush; there was far more land here than Jenny had realized. Beside an overhanging clump of trees was a warped and leaning toolshed.

"There," Angela said. "That's where P.C. went."

"Oh, no you don't." Jenny caught Dee in mid-lunge and held her back. "This isn't the time to be yanking doors open. Remember the Game?" She herself was trembling with anxiety, triumph, and anticipation.

Angela was fumbling with a large old-fashioned locket she had tucked into her tank top. "You need this to open it, anyway. I locked it again—afterward. It was our secret place, P.C.'s and mine. Nobody else wanted it."

Jenny took the key. "So you saw him go in that morning. And then . . . ?"

"Slug went in, too. P.C. climbed the porch and woke me up to get the key. That's my bedroom." She pointed to a second-story window above the porch roof. "Then he and Slug went down and unlocked the shed and went in. I could see everything from my room. I waited for them to come out—usually they just stashed stuff there and came out."

"But this time they didn't."

"No . . . so I waited and waited, then I got dressed. When I came down here, the door was still shut. So I opened it—but they weren't inside." She turned on Jenny suddenly, her dark eyes huge and brilliant with unshed tears. "They weren't inside! And there aren't any windows, and they didn't go out the door. And the key was on the ground. P.C. would never leave the key on the ground; he always locked up and gave it back to me. Where did they *go?*"

Jenny answered with a question. "There was something else on the ground, wasn't there? Besides the key?"

Angela nodded slowly.

"A . . ." Jenny took a breath. "A paper house."

"Yeah. A baby thing. It wasn't even new, it was kind of crumpled, and it was taped up with electrician's tape from the shed. I don't know why they took it. They usually took stuff like—" She broke off.

Dee cut a glance at Jenny, amused at the admission.

"It doesn't matter," Jenny said. "At least we know everything now. And it should still be inside if this place has been locked ever since that morning."

Angela nodded. "I didn't touch anything, even though—well, I sort of wanted to look at the house. But I didn't; I left it there on the floor. And nobody else has a key."

"Then let's go get it," Jenny said. Deep inside she was shaking. The paper house was here. They'd found it—and no wonder it had eluded them so long, sitting in a locked toolshed used by juvenile delinquents for hiding stolen goods.

"Monster positions?" Dee suggested with a flash of white teeth. She was clearly enjoying this.

"Right." Jenny took up a position beside the door. Dee stood in front of it in a kung fu stance, ready to kick it shut. It was the way they'd learned to open doors in the paper house. "Stand back, Angela. You, too, Cam."

"Now." Jenny turned the key, pulled the door open.

Nothing frightening happened. A rectangle of sunlight fell into the dusty shed. Jenny blocked it off with her own shadow as she stepped into the doorway. Then she moved inside, and Dee blocked the light.

"Come on in—I can't see—"

Then she did see—and her mind reeled.

The blank white box was on the floor, open. Beside it was the paper house Jenny had described to the police. A Victorian house, three stories and a turret. Blue.

Dee made a guttural sound.

When Jenny had last seen the paper house, it had been crushed flat to fit in the box. It was different now. It had been straightened and reenforced with black tape. But that wasn't what made Jenny's head spin and her breath catch. That wasn't what made her knees start to give way.

The paper house was exploded.

In shreds. Roof gone. Outer walls in tatters. Floors gutted.

As if something very large had burst out from the inside.

On the floor nearby, scratched impossibly deep into the concrete, was a mark. The rune Uruz. A letter from a magical alphabet, a spell to pierce the veil between the worlds. Jenny had seen it before on the inside of the box that had led them into the Shadow World. It was shaped like an angular and inverted *U,* with one stroke shorter than the other.

Right now she was looking at it upside-down, so that it should have looked like a regular *U.* But this particular rune was *very* uneven, the short stroke *very* short. From where she was standing it looked almost like a squared-off *J*.

Like a signature.

Even as Jenny turned toward Dee, she felt herself falling.

"We're too late," she whispered. "He's out."

"Okay," Dee said, some minutes later, still holding her. "Okay, okay . . ."

"It's *not* okay." She saw Cam and Angela peering in the doorway, and her head cleared a bit. "You two get back."

They came forward. "Is that it? What you've been looking for?" Cam squatted by the ruined house, his eyes as large and blue as Summer's. Light from the doorway made his dandelion hair glow at the edges. "What happened to it?"

Angela's dark eyes were huge—and despairing. "What happened to P.C.?"

Jenny looked at the house. It was gutted, every floor shredded. Her eyes filled again and she swallowed.

"I think he's probably dead," she said softly. "I'm sorry." The sight of Angela's misery cleared her head a little, brought her out of herself.

"Are you going to tell the police? About P.C. and me and this place?"

"The police," Jenny said bleakly, "are useless. We've learned that. There's nothing they can do. Maybe nothing *anybody* can do—" She stopped as an idea came to her. A desperate hope. "Angela, you said you didn't touch anything here—but are you sure? You didn't see anything on the floor, did you—like any jewelry?"

Angela shook her head. Jenny searched for it anyway. It had been inside the box; maybe it had just rolled away. It wouldn't make the police believe them, but it might just save her—if they could find it and destroy it—

She looked in the opened box and all around on the concrete floor. She shook out the ruins of the paper house.

But it wasn't anywhere. The gold ring that Julian had put on her finger, the one she tried to throw away, was gone.

8

What can we do?"

They were at Audrey's house, in the second-best family room where no adults would disturb them. Michael was looking at Jenny, his spaniel eyes glazed.

"Well, that's the question, isn't it?" Zachary said crisply. "What *can* we do?"

"I don't know," Jenny whispered.

The paper house—or rather its remains—sat on the coffee table. Jenny had brought it with them, to keep it safe. Although what they were going to do with it, she had no idea.

She'd taken both Angela and Cam by the hand before they left Angela's house. Scared as she was, she wanted to thank them—and to give them what comfort she could.

"I know it wasn't easy to help us," she said. "Now you need to forget all about this, if you can. We're the ones who have to take care of it. But I'll always remember what you've done—both of you."

Then she and Angela, the soshe and the Crying Girl, had hugged.

Outside, on Filbert Street, she and Dee had found Tom. His RX-7 was parked behind Dee's jeep. Clearly, he'd been following them, although Jenny still didn't understand why.

Now he sat beside Jenny, his hazel eyes thoughtful. "You know, I don't think they'll hurt *you*," he said to her. The emphasis on the last word was slight but noticeable.

"What do you mean, *they?*"

"The wolf and the snake. What did Julian call them? The Lurker and the Creeper."

Everyone stared.

"Tom, what are you talking about?"

"They're out, too. It was the wolf that followed you and Audrey on Monday. The Shadow Wolf. I only got a glimpse of it that night, but it wasn't a dog."

Audrey choked. "I've got *wolf* scratches on my car?"

"And that snake—I think maybe it's been around, too."

Jenny shut her eyes, remembering the dry sliding on the computer room floor. The brush against her leg. The hiss.

"Oh, God—then it's all been *real*," she said. "And the phone calls—oh, my God, oh, my *God*. They were *real*. They really were saying—" She couldn't finish.

"Models in your brain, my ass," Dee said to Michael.

Michael looked wretched. He bent his head, clutching his rumpled hair with his hands.

"And the dreams?" Audrey said thinly. "You think they were real, too? There was some—thing—in my bed with me?"

"Sounds like," Zach said, with morbid satisfaction. "Or maybe Julian can just make us dream what he wants."

"We have to do *something*," Dee said.

"Like what?" Zach's gray eyes shone with devastating logic. "What can we do against Julian? Plus that snake and that wolf. Don't you remember what they looked like?"

"I think they're the ones who got Gordie Wilson, incidentally," Tom said quietly. "I went up to the place where they found him."

"Oh, great. We don't have a chance," Michael said.

"Look, we're all in shock now," Dee said. "Let's get together this weekend at somebody's house and make plans. We can spend all Saturday thinking."

"At Tom's, maybe," Michael said. "I'm going to be there anyway; my dad's going to New York for a week."

Audrey looked at Jenny, then at Tom. Her camellia skin was pink, and she rubbed at her spiky lashes with one hand.

"I hate to say this, but we can't," she said. "At least Jenny and I can't. You're forgetting about the senior prom."

Tom looked up. ". . . *What?*"

"Jenny and I," Audrey said helplessly, "are going to the senior prom."

"With Brian Dettlinger and Eric Rankin," Michael said, in a misery-loves-company voice.

Tom was staring at Jenny. His face was perfectly white, and the green flecks in his eyes seemed to flare. Something seemed to have gone wrong with his mouth—it was trembling. Jenny looked back at him in absolute horror, her mind a thundering blank.

Then Tom said, slowly, "I see."

"No," Jenny whispered, stricken. She had never seen Tom look like this. Not when his grandmother died, not even when his father had had a heart attack. Tom Locke the invulnerable didn't have a face like that.

"It's okay. I should have expected it." He got up.

"Tom—"

"You ought to be safe enough. Like I said, I don't think they'll hurt *you.*"

"Tom—oh, God, *Tom—*"

He was walking out the door.

Jenny whirled on Audrey and Michael, lashing out in her misery. "Are you happy now? You made him leave!"

"Do you think that means he doesn't want me for the weekend?" Michael asked, but Dee spoke seriously.

"He wasn't really here, Jenny. He's not with us anymore, Sunshine, and you can't make him be."

Jenny waited a moment while Dee's words slowly sank in. It was true. There was no way to deny it. Jenny hadn't lost anything just now, because she had nothing left to lose.

She sat down and said dully, "Obviously not. And somehow I don't think going to the prom with Brian is going to help, either." She looked at Audrey.

Audrey, however, refused to be fazed. "Who

knows? He might feel differently when he sees you actually doing it."

"I'm not *going* to be doing it."

"So you're going to call Brian and dump him at the last minute?"

"Yes." Jenny fumbled in her purse for her address book. She went to Audrey's gold-and-white antique phone and dialed.

"Hello, Brian? It's Jenny—"

"Jenny! I'm so glad you called."

Jenny faltered. "You are?"

"Yeah, I was going to call you—look, I'm so stupid. I forgot to ask you what color your dress is."

"My dress?"

"I know I should have asked before." His voice was full of eagerness and—oh, God—boyish enthusiasm. "It's not that I haven't been thinking about you. The limo's all lined up, and I made reservations at L'Avenue—do you like French food?"

"Oh . . ." Jenny felt limp as seaweed. "Oh . . . sure."

"Great. And your dress is what color?"

Audrey had come over and was leaning her copper head close to the earpiece. "Tell him gold," she whispered.

"Gold," Jenny repeated automatically, then looked at Audrey. "Oh, no, not that one," she whispered fiercely.

"What? Gold's great. I'll see you tomorrow."

Jenny hung up dazedly. She hadn't been able to do it.

"You see?" Audrey said grimly. "I'm stuck, too. Stop looking like that, Michael. I don't care about Eric—much."

Dee stretched. "When you get down to it, what difference does it make where you are? They can get into our houses if they want."

It was true. It wasn't much comfort. Jenny still didn't see how she could go—or how she could get out of it now.

"I can't wear *that* dress," she said to Audrey. "Tom wouldn't even let me wear it with *him*. If he hears I wore it with Brian, he'll have a fit. . . ." Her voice trailed off as new hope ignited suddenly in her chest.

Audrey smiled knowingly. "Then maybe," she said archly, "the prom will do some good after all."

Jenny picked up the handful of liquid gold, put it down again. She couldn't believe she was doing this.

On the other hand, Dee was right. What difference did it make where Jenny was? There was nowhere safe. At least the Monarch Hotel was a large public place. She and Audrey would be surrounded by people.

Last night and today had been very quiet. No dreams, no disturbances. The calm before the storm? Or maybe . . . maybe some miracle had happened and all the bad things had gone away. Spontaneously popped back into the Shadow World. Maybe Julian was going to leave her alone from now on.

Don't be ridiculous, Jenny.

She sighed and shook her head. Too much worrying had sapped her energy and put her in a fatalistic mood.

She picked up the liquid gold again. It was the Dress.

The material was gold foil, which showed a subtle pattern of flowers and leaves when the light hit it the right way—almost like tapestry. The colors were rich and shimmering, and the thin fabric was silky-soft. Audrey had been crazy over it, but Audrey only wore black and white.

"You *have* to get it," she'd told Jenny, tilting the shining fabric back and forth under the lights and ignoring the bevy of trailing saleswomen— saleswomen always trailed when Audrey shopped.

"But Tom—"

"Forget Tom. When are you going to stop letting him tell you what to wear? *You must buy this dress.* With your gold-y skin and hair it will be *exquisite.*"

So Jenny had bought it. But she'd been right; Tom wouldn't let her wear it to the junior prom. It was too short, too clinging, molding itself to her like a shining skin. Her legs looked as long as Dee's underneath.

Now she put it on and reached for a brush. She bent over, brushing, then stood, flipping her hair back. She ran her fingers through her hair to fluff it.

Then she stepped to the full-length maple mirror. She had to admit it; the dress was a masterpiece. A glittering, shameless work of art. Her hair was a mass of dark gold around her face, different from her usual soft look. Her entire image seemed touched with gold.

She looked like a crown princess. She felt like a virgin sacrifice.

"Jenny." Her mother was tapping at her bedroom door. "He's here."

Jenny stared at herself for another moment hopelessly. "Right," she said and came out.

Brian's jaw dropped when he saw her. So, unfortunately, did Mr. Thornton's.

"Jim, now, Jim," her mother said. She led Jenny's father off into the kitchen, talking to him about how responsible Jenny was and how Brian's mother was a member of the Assistance League.

"Are those my flowers?" Jenny said, since Brian was still gaping at her. He held out the corsage box dumbly.

The plastic was clouded with mist, but when Jenny opened it, she saw an ethereal bunch of palest lemon miniature roses. "But they're beautiful!"

"Uh. Um." Brian blinked at the flowers, then shook his head slightly. He took them out, looked at her low neckline. He reached toward her doubtfully, pulled back. "Uh . . ."

"I'll do it," Jenny said and fastened them on her shoulder. Then she put on his boutonniere and they left.

The limo was champagne-colored, and they weren't sharing it with anybody. Brian looked nice, blond and handsome, with a royal blue cummerbund and tie. All the way to the restaurant Jenny concentrated on the tiny shiny buttons on his tux in order to keep from crying.

She'd never been out with any boy besides Tom.

Dinner was uneventful. Brian was awed by everything she said and did, which made him easy to get along with. He wasn't smart like Tom, but he was a nice guy. A really nice guy.

Palm trees lined the private drive of the hotel. It was a beautiful and dreamlike setting, a cliff above the sea. Mercedes and Cadillacs were parked everywhere and bellhops in red uniforms were running around.

As Jenny got out of the limo, she began to realize something. The senior prom was like a junior prom some fairy godmother had waved a wand over. Everything grander, bigger, more glittery. More grown-up. It was scary, but kind of wonderful.

They walked between marble columns into an enchanted world. Acres of Italian marble. Huge urns of flowers—all arranged in exquisitely simple good taste. Persian carpets, silk wallcoverings, Bohemian crystal chandeliers.

Audrey must be loving this, Jenny thought, stopping somewhere along the miles of hallway to look at an oil painting.

When they finally reached the ballroom, Jenny drew in her breath.

It was . . . fabulous. In the old sense, meaning like something out of a fable. Like a castle. The ceilings were incredibly high, with huge chandeliers in deep recesses. Potted trees—full-size trees entwined with tiny lights—stood here and there among the tables. At one end of the room poufy curtains were drawn back to reveal a balcony, which Jenny guessed looked down on the ocean.

"It's beautiful," Jenny breathed, forgetting everything for a moment.

"It sure is." When she looked, Brian was looking at her.

The tables were as incredible as everything else. There were fresh flowers in blown-glass stands that reached above Jenny's head when she was sitting down. At each place was a little metallic mask as a favor.

"The Midnight Masquerade," Brian said, holding

97

a silver one up to his eyes. "Don't put yours on, though; you're too pretty without it."

Jenny looked away.

"These flowers are beautiful," she said hastily. They were. The roses had a pale gold shimmer unlike anything she'd ever seen, and they smelled so sweet it almost made her giddy.

"Yeah, well, I have to confess—I can't take the credit for them. I ordered white ones for Ka—I mean, I ordered plain white ones. The florist must have screwed up, but it turned out great."

Jenny stirred. For some reason prickles of unease were touching her delicately.

Just then some of Brian's friends came by. One of them stared at Jenny, blinked, then whispered something to Brian that ended with "I bet *you're* planning to stay out late!"

Brian blushed. Jenny leaned across him and said directly to the other guy, *"Vada via, cretino."* Audrey had taught her that. It meant "Get lost, jerk," and it sounded like it.

The guy left, muttering, "And I heard she was sweet!"

Brian, still blushing was embarrassed and apologetic. A nice guy, Jenny thought, feeling sorry for him. A really, really nice guy. . . .

They talked. Jenny looked at the snowy-white tablecloth and the shining crystal glasses, she played with her prom program and her raffle ticket. She stared at the Oriental border of the carpet. Finally, though, there was no way to avoid the subject that was looming over both of them.

"You want to dance?" Brian said.

What could she say?

Okay, she thought as they walked onto the floor. It's not as if you've never danced with another guy before. But she hadn't, often. Tom didn't like it. Besides, she'd always been *with* Tom, and the guy had always known it.

Naturally, the next dance turned out to be a slow one. The room was just dim enough to be romantic. Brian's arms settled around Jenny's shoulders, and Jenny clasped his waist as lightly as possible. She rested her head on his chest and looked intently at the refreshment table.

It was a marble-topped buffet with huge urns of flowers on either side. Jenny concentrated on identifying the flowers, one by one. Then she saw a glimmer of burnished copper.

"Look, there's *Audrey!*" she said. "Let's go see her!"

Audrey was wearing a saucy little black dress with a pink satin sash at the back. Diamonds glittered in her ears. Her chestnut eyes widened at the sight of Jenny.

"Will you look at you! Jenny, you're sensational. *Wunderschön!*"

Jenny clung to Audrey and made wild small talk. Other people went by. She saw dresses in every color of the rainbow; she saw lime green cummerbunds and pink cummerbunds and plaid ones. But at last Eric and Audrey went out to dance, and Jenny had no choice but to follow with Brian.

When the next slow dance came, she rested stiffly in Brian's arms, staring at the dark wood of the dance floor.

He was too interested. Jenny had seen it all night: the look in his eyes, the way he held her, the way he talked to her. He was such a nice guy, so handsome, and she felt *nothing*.

"Later we can go down to the beach," he was saying.

"Mmm," Jenny said, thinking that she had to get away from the smell of his lime aftershave, and hating herself for it. She wished desperately that someone would rescue her.

Someone did.

It was another guy, and he wanted to cut in. Jenny tried to hide her gratitude as she transferred herself to the new guy's shoulder. He looked like a senior, although she didn't recognize him because he was actually wearing one of those thematic little masks. A black one.

Jenny didn't care who he was. He'd saved her from Brian, and from her guilt at coming with Brian under false pretenses. She saw now that she was going to have to apologize to Brian before tonight was over, apologize and explain everything. He'd probably hate her. He'd probably leave her stranded at the hotel. Jenny kind of hoped he would; it would make her feel better.

The new guy held her very lightly. Jenny floated in his arms and let her mind drift back to junior prom. She had worn ivory lace, soft and romantic and old-fashioned, the kind Tom liked. Audrey had worn a different classic black dress. Summer had been in pale aquamarine, with fringe all over, like a flapper. Tom had looked wonderful in severe black and white. Afterward they'd all gone to McDonald's in their fancy clothes, laughing and fooling around. It had been a wonderful night because they'd been together.

Now here she was in fairyland, surrounded by strangers.

That thought was a little disturbing.

She and the new guy had swayed a little away from the other dancers. He actually seemed to know something about dancing, or at least he was semimobile. It was darker here near the balcony. Jenny felt strangely isolated.

And—it was curious, but everything seemed to have slowed. The music had changed. The band seemed to have segued into another slow dance, a haunting melody by some female vocalist Jenny knew but couldn't put her finger on at the moment. Otherworldly. Weird of them to do that without giving people a chance to change partners.

Weird melody, too, but beautiful. It was music that got into your blood, that made you feel strange.

Jenny was feeling very strange.

Time seemed to be stretching.

She didn't want to look up, because that was bad manners unless you wanted to be kissed. And Jenny didn't, whatever kind of music it was. Safer just to keep her head down.

They were on the threshold of the balcony now, and Jenny could look out over it onto the ocean. It was even darker here, so you could see the ocean below. Spotlights reflected off the water, looking like a handful of moons.

Oddly, there was no one on the balcony. Jenny would have thought it would have been crammed body-to-body, but there was nobody here—or at least nobody she could see in the dark. Her partner was leading her toward the darkest corner.

I shouldn't go. . . . Oh, God, I'm going to have to say Vada via, cretino *again. . . .*

But she couldn't seem to resist.

Here on the balcony she could feel the night air, just faintly cool on her arms and the back of her neck. The music seemed distant. She could no longer make out words, only single notes, pure and clear as drops of water falling into a still pool. Falling slowly. Jenny had the queer feeling that she herself was falling.

As loud as the music was the roar of the ocean. They were near the edge of the balcony now. The waves were hissing and crashing on the beach below. An eerie sound, Jenny thought, her mind strangely muddled. A formless, featureless, endless sound. Like white noise . . .

Shhshhshhshhshhshhshh.

All at once she was awake. Awake, with chills sweeping over her and icy terror in her stomach. Not only her little fingers but the sides of her hands were tingling.

Get out of here!

Then, at last, she tried to pull away. But her partner wouldn't let her. She was held in a grip of steel. One of his arms was trapping her arms, the other was holding the back of her head.

She couldn't move. There was no question of screaming. She was alone with him on the balcony, separated by what seemed like miles from the rest of the dance. She could no longer hear any music, only wind in the palm trees and the ocean crashing below. They were very close to a very long drop.

She could see a strand of her partner's hair now, above a shirt collar as black as his tux. She hadn't realized that before—he was all in black and his hair was blond. Blonder than Brian's, blonder even than Cam's. Almost white—

—as white as frost or icicles or mist, as white as winter—

—as white as death—

A voice whispered in her ear, *"Famished."*

Not like that. Longer. *"Faaamishhshhed . . ."*

9

Everything went gray.

Blood roared in Jenny's ears like the ocean. She was thrown back, in one instant, to the moment when she and Tom and the others had been sucked into the Game, dragged into the Shadow World. She felt the same riptide dragging at her now, the same dark fog overcoming her senses. The same mindless, helpless terror. She was falling into the emptiness.

She didn't faint. She wished she could, but she didn't. She hung in his arms, barely supporting her own weight, feeling darkness all around her, and remained conscious.

He was going to kill her. He was the voice on the phone. He'd sent the Shadow Wolf after her and Audrey, he'd sent the snake after her in computer class. He'd killed Gordie Wilson.

She could still hear the distorted, malign whisper in her head: *"Famished . . ."*

Jenny sobbed.

Sheer terror gave her the strength to take her own weight again, to try and get free again. To her astonishment, he let her. She reeled backward two steps and came up against the balcony railing. Then she just stared at him.

Her first thought was that she should have been more prepared—but there was no way to prepare for Julian. He was always a shock to the senses.

His eyes behind the black mask were like liquid cobalt. His entire face was shadowed. His hair shone in the dimness, as white as moonlight on water.

He wasn't like a human. He was sharper, fiercer, brighter than any human could be. More *real*— which was strange, since *this* was supposed to be the real world.

He was in her world now, not even in some halfway place like the More Games store which seemed to exist between the worlds. He was here, walking around, capable of *anything*.

And just now he radiated menace. Danger.

Jenny's heart was beating so hard and erratically that she thought she might shatter.

"Yellow roses mean infidelity, you know," he said casually.

She remembered his voice now. Once away from it, she'd forgotten. She'd only remembered what she'd *thought* about it, which was that it was musical and elemental, like water running over rock, but that didn't really give any sense of its beauty—or its coldness.

She put a hand to the cluster of miniature roses at her shoulder. The lovely pale flowers with their golden sheen. In her mind she saw Brian blinking at the sight of them, heard him saying, *"The florist must have screwed up. . . . "*

"You sent them," she said. Her voice came out oddly—choked and so openly frightened that she was ashamed. She wanted to tear the roses off, but her hands were shaking.

"Of course. Didn't you know?"

She should have known, but she'd been too stupid. All night she'd been too stupid. She had gone off with a boy in a mask because he didn't look like Julian, forgetting that Julian could look like anyone he wanted. Or *had* she forgotten? Maybe some part of her had known, and had wanted to get it over with. She'd been so frightened for so long.

With good reason. The last time she'd been with Julian, she'd betrayed him. She'd lied to him, made him believe her—maybe even trust her. And then she'd slammed a door on him, meaning to trap him behind it forever. She'd left him imprisoned like a genie in a bottle. She could only imagine what he must have felt when he realized what she'd done. Now he'd come for his revenge.

"Why don't you just do it?" she said. She was more pleased with her voice this time; it was clear, if not quite steady. She'd die with dignity. "Go ahead and kill me."

He tilted his silvery-blond head slightly. "Is that what I want to do?" he said.

"It's what you did to Gordie Wilson."

He smiled—oh, God, she'd forgotten that smile. Wolf-hungry. The sort of smile to send you running and screaming—or to make you collapse in a heap on the floor.

"Not personally," he said.

"But it's what you brought me here for, isn't it?" Jenny glanced back at the drop behind her. Her fragile composure was splintering. Hysteria was bubbling up inside her, and she couldn't stop it. If he wasn't going to throw her over, then maybe she ought to jump, because dying fast would be better than whatever he *was* going to do with her. . . . "Just go ahead and *do* it. Just get it over with."

"All right," he said, and kissed her.

Oh.

She'd thought she remembered how it was with Julian, how it felt to be kissed by him. Her memories had lied. Or maybe this kind of thing was too strong for memory to be anything but a shadow of it. In one instant she was transported back to the paper house, back to the shock she'd felt at his first touch. When Tom held her—back in the old days, when Tom still loved her—his arms had made her feel safe. Comforted.

Julian didn't make her feel safe at all. She was trembling instantly. Falling. Soaring. The electricity he carried around with him flooding into her, tingling in every nerve ending. Sweet shocks that sent her mind reeling.

Oh, God, I *can't*—it's wrong. It's wrong, he's *evil*. I can't feel anything for him. I told Tom I didn't feel anything. . . .

Her body didn't listen to her.

He wants to *kill* me. . . .

But he was kissing her as softly as twilight, tiny sweet kisses and long ones that turned wild. As if they were lovers reunited, instead of hunter and prey.

And Jenny was kissing him back. Her arms were around his neck. He changed the pressure of his lips on hers and light flashed through her. She opened her eyes in shock.

"Jenny," Julian said, not moving away, speaking with his lips brushing hers. He sounded glad— exalted. Full of discovery. "You see how it is with us? You can't fight it any more than I can. You've tried; you've done everything you can to kill it. But you can't kill my love for you."

"No," Jenny whispered. His face was so close, the mask making him look more dangerous than ever. He was terrifying—and beautiful. She couldn't look away from him.

"We were meant to be together. It's our destiny. You've put up a good fight, but it's over now. Give in, Jenny. Let me love you."

"No!" With sudden strength she pushed him— hard. Shoving him away. The force sent her backward against the railing.

Fury swept over his face. Then it ebbed and he sighed deeply. "You're going to fight to the end, aren't you? All right. You're exciting when you're angry, and personally I'm starved for the sight of you. In fact, you might say I'm famished—"

"Don't."

"I like the dress," he continued, as if she hadn't spoken. "In a purely aesthetic sense, of course. And I like your hair like that. It makes you look wild and beautiful."

Terrifyingly, Jenny felt wild and beautiful. Felt desirable. It wasn't right, but his eyes on her made her feel as if no one had ever been as beautiful as she was, since the beginning of time.

108

But she never stopped feeling frightened, either.

He took her hand. She felt—not saw, because she couldn't take her eyes from his—something slip onto her finger. A cold circlet. A ring. She felt the chill of it all around her as if she'd been banded with ice.

The gold ring she'd thrown away.

Julian said, as if quoting:

"This ring, the symbol of my oath,
Will hold me to the words I speak:
All I refuse and thee I choose."

Jenny shut her eyes.

"Don't you remember? I told you the promise was irrevocable. You are sworn mine, Jenny. Now and forever."

If Darkness had taken on a face and a voice, if the powers of night had gathered themselves together and formed themselves into a human being, they would have made something like Julian.

And she was his.

Like some horrible old movie, yes. Bride of the Devil. She'd promised herself to him, and now she had no choice.

Or at least some part of her believed that. A part of her she hadn't even known existed before she'd met Julian. A part that had changed her recently, so that people noticed. The wild part, a part that craved risks. Like the thing in Dee that loved danger.

It was this part that responded to him, that found the rest of the world tame by comparison. The part that made her heart pound and her stomach melt. Her knees literally felt weak—the way they had after the last big earthquake in L.A., when the ground did things solid ground wasn't supposed to do, when she'd thought she was going to die. Afterward, her legs had actually felt like wax. The way they did now.

"I've only come to claim what's mine. You cast your own fate, Jenny, you doomed yourself. That's the way it works with runes and oaths. You spoke the words, you let them be written, and that's it. Didn't you ever think you'd have to make good?"

Jenny didn't know what she'd thought. She'd done it to save Tom and the others—she would have done anything to save them at that point.

"It was—I couldn't—it wasn't *fair*," she said, fumbling. She was at a disadvantage; she couldn't think properly.

"Fair—let's not get on that again. Life isn't fair. That's not the point. You promised yourself to me."

Jenny opened her mouth to explain, but she couldn't seem to summon up any words.

Because the terrible thing was that he was right. There was no real way to justify what she'd done. She'd given him her word. She'd sworn the oath, knowing it would bind her forever. And she supposed the shameful truth was that she'd hoped to get rid of Julian so that he couldn't collect.

With one finger Julian sketched some lines in the air, a shape like a vase turned on its side. "That's Perthro, the rune of gambling and divination. It's the cup that holds the runes or dice when they're cast."

"Oh, really?" Jenny said weakly, not having the first idea what he was talking about.

"I'll tell you something interesting about the people who discovered those runes. They loved gambling. Crazy about it. They would bet everything—

including their freedom—on one throw of the dice. And if they lost, they'd go into slavery cheerfully, because they had made a promise and they always played by the rules. Honor meant more than anything to them."

Jenny looked away, hugging her own arms. She felt very cold. She wished there were somewhere to hide.

"Are you going to keep your promise?"

What could she say? That it was a promise she never should have had to make? Julian had forced her to play the Game in the beginning—but Jenny had come to him looking for a game. Looking for something scary and sexy, something to provide excitement at a party. Julian had just given her what she'd asked for. It was her own fault for meddling with forbidden things.

But she couldn't—she *couldn't*.

Teeth sunk into her lower lip, she looked at Julian. She could hardly meet his eyes, but she did. She shook her head.

There. Now it was out. She didn't have any excuses, but she wasn't going to keep her word.

"You know I could just make you."

She nodded. It was what she expected. But at least she wouldn't have gone to him willingly.

He turned to look down at the ocean, and Jenny waited.

"What do you say we play another game?"

"Oh, *no*," Jenny whispered, but he was going on.

"I could just force you—but I'll give you a sporting chance. One throw of the dice, Jenny. One more game. If you win, you're free of the promise. If you lose, you keep it." He turned back to look at her, and in the eyeholes of the mask she could see midnight

111

blue. "Do you want to play, or do we just resolve this here and now?

Don't panic—*think*. It's your only chance. It's better than no chance.

And the wild part in her was responding to his challenge, surging to meet it. Danger. Risk. Excitement.

"One throw of the dice," she said softly. "I'll play."

He flashed her the wolfish smile. "No holds barred, then. No quarter asked or given—for any of the players."

Jenny froze. "Wait a minute—" she began.

"Did you think I was going to fool around? This game is deadly serious—like the last one."

"But it's between *us*," Jenny said desperately. "Just you and me—"

"No." The eyes behind the mask were narrow. "This is a game for the original players, for everyone who was in the paper house. No more and no less. On my side, myself and the Creeper and the Lurker. On your side—everyone who helped trick me and betray me. I'm going to catch them one by one, starting with Little Red Riding-Hood."

"No," Jenny said, in terror. Oh, God, what had she done? Summer had *died* in the last Game. . . .

"Yes. And it starts now. Ready or not, here I come. Find my base and you can stop me from taking them to the Shadow World."

"Taking *who*—?"

"Your friends. Find them after I take them and you all go free. If not"—he smiled—"I keep them all."

Jenny didn't understand. Panic was rioting inside

her. She wasn't ready—she didn't know the rules. She didn't even know what game they were playing.

"Julian—"

Quick as a cat, quick as a striking snake, he kissed her. A hard kiss, and Jenny was responding before she knew it.

When it was over, he held her tightly to his chest a moment. She could hear his heart beating—just like a human heart, she thought dizzily. Then he whispered in her ear, "The new game is lambs and monsters." And he was gone.

Gone from the balcony, just like that. The warmth dissolved from Jenny's arms, and she was standing alone.

She could hear the music again. It might all have been a dream, but she could still feel Julian's hard kiss on her mouth.

The shadows on the balcony had lightened in his absence. Jenny looked around fearfully. Julian had said that the Game would start now. Julian didn't say things he didn't mean.

But she couldn't see anything unusual. The dance was going on inside the ballroom. Jenny turned and gripped the railing of the balcony, looking over.

Spotlights softly lit the beach below. One of them caught the glint of copper.

Audrey! That was Audrey down there, and the dark-haired figure beside her must be Eric. They were yards away from the other people on the sand, walking hand in hand down the beach. Into the darkness.

The Game starts now. . . . I'm going to catch them one by one, starting with Little Red Riding-Hood.

Red—like Audrey's hair.

"Audrey! *Audrey!*" Jenny screamed. Her voice disappeared into the background of music without even a ripple. She could feel how small and faint it was compared to the roaring of the ocean. Jenny looked around wildly; there was no way from the balcony down to the beach.

Audrey and Eric were walking out of the range of the lights now, heading into the shadows.

"Audrey!"

Audrey didn't hear her.

Something about dances always went to Audrey's head.

For instance, she didn't really like Eric, the boy she was presently kissing. She just couldn't help it—something about dances got to her. All the lights—and the dark corners. The sparkly dresses and the compliments and the music. It was better than shopping.

And Eric was a pretty good kisser, for an American boy.

Not as good as Michael, though. Michael Cohen was a world-class kisser, although you'd never think it to look at him. It was one of the best-kept secrets at Vista Grande High, and Audrey meant it to remain that way.

She felt a slight twinge of guilt, thinking of Michael. Well, but she'd told him she didn't care about Eric. She was doing it to help Jenny.

Who was up in the hotel trying to deal with Brian and his unwanted attentions. Maybe it was time Audrey did something about that.

"Eric," she said, detaching herself and neatening her hair. "We'd better get back."

He started to protest, but Audrey was already turning. She hadn't realized how far they'd walked away from the lights of the hotel.

"Come on," she said uneasily.

She had only taken a few steps when she caught movement out of the corner of her eye. It was on her left, on the land side. Something in the shadows, a quick bright flicker.

Maybe just some small animal or bird. "Eric, come on."

He was sulking. "You go, if you want to."

Oh, fine. She began walking as quickly as she could. Her bare feet sank with each step into the soft, crumbly, faintly damp sand.

The hotel spotlights seemed miles away. The ocean stretched out to her right, unimaginably vast. To her left darkness blanketed a slope covered with ice plant. Between the darkness and the sea, Audrey felt small and vulnerable in comparison. It was a bad feeling.

She turned suddenly and looked into the darkness. She couldn't see anything now. Maybe nothing was there.

Then she heard a cry behind her. Audrey whirled, straining to see in the darkness. Something was going on back there—some kind of activity.

"Eric? Eric!"

Another cry. And, louder, a terrible sound that Audrey could hear over the ocean. A guttural, vibrating snarl. A bestial noise.

Sand was spraying. Audrey could see some kind of thrashing. *"Eric!* Eric, what's happening?"

The thrashing had stopped. Audrey took an uncertain step forward. "Eric?"

Something glimmered, coming toward her.

Not Eric. Something blue and shining. Like an optical illusion, there and then gone. Audrey tried to make her eyes focus—and the lost time was fatal. By the time she saw it clearly it was almost on her.

Oh, God—it was unbelievable. In the Shadow World the wolf had looked like a wolf. Huge, massive, but just a wolf. This thing . . . was a phantom.

Like something painted with luminous paint on the air. Nothing in between the brush strokes. Not exactly a skeleton—something worse. A specter. A wraith-wolf.

The growling was real.

Audrey turned and ran.

It was right behind her. She could hear its growling over the roar of the ocean, over her own sobbing breath. Her legs were beginning to ache already. The thick sand sucked at her, dragging her down. It was like running in slow motion.

She was closer to the lights. If she could just get there—but it was too far. She would never make it.

The ground opened up in front of her.

That was what it looked like. A hole, black against the gray sand. Black with flickering electric-blue edges.

The sand that had been her enemy helped her now, allowed her to catch herself and fall to her knees. She fell right on the brink of the hole, staring down in disbelief.

God—God. It was like nothing she had ever seen. Endless blackness forever. Down at the very bottom there might have been the shimmer of a blue flame.

Audrey didn't want to see any more. She staggered to her feet and ran toward the slope on her left. If she could climb up through the ice plant—maybe she could lose herself there.

But it was fast. It came up on her left side, cutting her off, forcing her to swerve. It turned with her, forcing her to swerve again. To circle back toward the hole.

Audrey stumbled again and heard a snarl right behind her. Hot breath on her neck.

She didn't have the breath to scream, although there was a screaming in her brain. She clawed her way up and was running again.

The way it wanted her to go. She realized that too late. The hole was in front of her, almost beneath her feet. She couldn't stop herself this time.

10

In midair she was knocked to the side with stunning force. A brutal blocking tackle. She landed with her face crushed into the sand. Not in the hole, on the beach.

Chaos was going on above her. On top of her. A whole football team scrimmaging there. Thick snarls, gasping breath, then suddenly a yelp. Sand fountained around her.

Then it all stopped.

Audrey lay still for a moment longer, then rolled over to look.

Tom was half sitting, half crouching in the sand, his dark hair wildly mussed, his face scratched. He was breathing in gasps. In his hand was a Swiss Army knife, the blade not shining but dark. The wolf was gone. So was the hole.

"Is it dead?" Audrey panted. She could hear the hysteria in her own voice.

"No. It went into that crater thing. Then the crater disappeared."

"Oh," Audrey said. She looked at him, blinked. "You know, we've got to stop meeting like this." Then she collapsed back on the sand.

"Audrey! Audrey, where are you? Audrey!"

Audrey had seldom heard a voice filled with so much terror, but she was drifting in an endorphin cloud of overexertion. She could barely rouse herself to wave a hand without looking.

"We're here!" Tom shouted. "Here!"

The next moment Jenny was on her knees beside them. "Oh, God, what happened? Are you all right?"

"The wolf happened," Tom said. "She's all right, it's just reaction."

"Are *you* all right? Oh, Tom, you're bleeding!"

Sounds of hugging. Normally, Audrey would have let them have their reunion in peace, but now she said, "Eric's back there. I don't know if he's all right."

"I'll go see." Tom detached himself from Jenny's arms and went. Jenny turned to Audrey, golden dress shining in the gloom.

"What happened?"

"It tried to chase me into a hole. A hole," she repeated, before Jenny could ask, and described the thing she'd seen. "I don't know why, but it wanted me to fall in."

"Oh, my God," Jenny whispered. "Oh, God, Audrey, it's all my fault. And if Eric is dead—"

"He's not dead," Tom said, coming back up. "He's breathing, and I can't even find any bleeding or anything. The wolf didn't want him; it wanted Audrey."

It was only then that Jenny asked, "What are you doing here?"

Tom looked at the ocean. "I didn't think anything would happen here—but I wasn't sure. I hung around in the hotel just in case. When I saw Audrey going down to the beach, I kept an eye on her from the deck up there."

"Oh, Tom," Jenny said again.

"Thank God you did," Audrey said, picking herself up. She was bruised, but everything seemed to be in working order. Her brand new Oscar de la Renta, though, was another matter. "It's a pity you couldn't have saved the dress, too."

As they climbed the sandy ocean ramp up to the hotel grounds, she said thoughtfully, "Actually, I suppose you saved my life. It doesn't really matter about the dress."

"We can't be the ones to tell the police about Eric," Jenny said. "Because we can't afford to lose the time, and because they might separate us. But we can't just leave him there, either."

There was a fine trembling in all her muscles, her reaction nearly as severe as Audrey's. Deep inside her, though, was a steel core of determination. She knew what had to be done.

"Why can't we lose the time?" Tom asked.

"Because we've got to get the others," Jenny said. "We all need to go somewhere and talk." She saw Audrey, who was slowly making repairs to her hair and dress, give her a sharp glance. "I'll explain later; for now just *trust me*, Tom."

Tom's hazel eyes were dark, puzzled, but after a

moment he nodded. "Let me get cleaned up a little; then I'll go tell them at the front desk that there's somebody unconscious on the beach. Then we can go."

When he went, he took a note to send up to the ballroom, too. It was from Jenny to Brian, explaining that she had to leave the prom without him, and that she was sorry.

Jenny shut her eyes and leaned against the wall. Think, she told herself. Don't collapse yet, think.

"Audrey, we both need to call our parents. We've got to tell them—something—some reason why we're not coming home tonight. And then we need to think of somewhere we can go. I wonder how much a hotel room costs?"

Audrey, with two bobby pins in her mouth, just looked at Jenny. She couldn't speak, but the look was enough.

"We're not doing anything dangerous," Jenny assured her. "But we've *got* to talk. And I think we'll only be safe when we're all together."

Audrey removed the pins and licked her lips. "What about Michael's apartment?" she said. "His dad's gone for the week."

"Audrey, you're brilliant. Now think of what we say to our parents, and we'll be fine."

In the end they settled for the old double-bluff. Jenny called her house and told her mother she would be staying at Audrey's; Audrey called her house and told Gabrielle the housekeeper that she would be staying at Jenny's. Then they called Dee, who had her own phone, and had her come out to the hotel in her jeep, while Tom took the RX-7 to his house to pick up Michael. Finally Tom went back out for Zach, while a cross and sleep-wrinkled Michael let the others into his apartment.

It was nearly one-thirty in the morning when they were all together.

"Caffeine," Michael mumbled. "For God's sake."

"Stunts your growth," said Dee. "Makes you blind."

"Why isn't there anything in this refrigerator except mayonnaise and Diet Coke?" Audrey called.

"There should be some cream cheese in there somewhere," Michael said. "And there's Cracker Jack in the cupboard; Dad bought a case at the Price Club. If you love me at all, bring me a Coke and tell me what's going on. I was asleep."

"And I nearly got killed," Audrey said, coming around the corner in time to see his eyes widen. "Here." She distributed Diet Cokes and Cracker Jack to everyone except Dee, who just snorted.

What a mismatched group we are, Jenny thought, looking around at them. Michael and Audrey were on the couch, Michael in the faded gray sweats he wore as pajamas, and Audrey in the ruins of her saucy little black dress. Dee was on the other side of Audrey, dressed for action in biking shorts and a khaki tank top, long legs sprawled in front of her.

Tom, on the love seat, was windblown and handsome in jeans and a dark blue jersey. Zach sat on the floor by the table wearing a vaguely Oriental black outfit—maybe pajamas, maybe a jogging suit, Jenny thought. Jenny herself was perched on the arm of the love seat in her shimmering and totally inappropriate gold dress. She hadn't thought about changing.

She could see Dee's eyes on the dress, but she

couldn't return the amused glance. She was too wrought-up.

"Isn't *somebody* going to explain what's going on?" Michael said, tearing into the Cracker Jack.

"Audrey can start," Jenny said, clasping her hands together and trying to keep them still.

Audrey quickly described what had happened.

"But what's with this hole?" Michael said when she finished. "Pardon me for asking, but how come the wolf didn't just kill you? If it's the same one that attacked Gordie Wilson."

"Because it's a Game," Jenny said. "A new Game."

Dee's piercing night-dark gaze was on her. "You've seen Julian," she said without hesitation.

Jenny nodded, clenching her hands even more tightly together. Tom turned to look at her sharply, then turned away, his shoulders tense. Zach stared at her with an inscrutable expression, the black outfit accentuating his pallor. Michael whistled.

Audrey, her back very straight, said, "Tell us."

Jenny told them. Not everything, but the essence of what had happened, leaving out the bits that nobody needed to know. Like the kissing.

"He said that he'd give me a chance to get free of my promise," she finished. "That he was going to play a new Game with us, and that we were all players. And at the end he said that the new Game was lambs and monsters."

Audrey drew in her breath, frowning. "Like that thing we saw those kids playing?"

"*What* lambs and monsters?" Michael demanded. "I never heard of it."

"It's like cops and robbers," Jenny said. "It starts

like hide-and-seek—if you're the monster, you count while all the lambs hide. Then when you find a lamb, you chase it—and if you tag it, it's caught. Then you bring it back to your base and keep it as a prisoner until somebody else sneaks up to let it free."

"Or until all the lambs are caught and they get eaten," Audrey said darkly.

"Cute game," said Zach, then relapsed into silence.

"If we're playing, we'd better figure out the rules," Dee said.

"We may not have to play," Jenny said.

They all looked at her. She knew she was flushed. She had been thinking ever since she'd looked over the balcony railing to see Audrey's tiny figure disappear into darkness, and by now she'd worked herself into a rather odd state.

"What do you mean?" Dee said, lynx-eyed.

Jenny heard herself give a strange little overstrained laugh. "Well, maybe I should just stop it right now."

She was surprised by the volume of the protest.

"No!" Audrey cried. "Give in to a guy—any guy? Absolutely not. Never."

"We have to fight him," Dee said, smacking a slender fist into her palm. "You know that, Jenny."

"We're *going* to fight him," Tom said grimly.

"Uh, look," Michael said, and then got Audrey's elbow in his ribs. "I mean—you'd better not."

"That's right, you'd *better* not," Audrey said. "And I'm the one who got chased tonight, so I'm the one who's got the right to say it."

"We won't *let* you," Dee said, both long legs on the

124

floor now, leaning forward in the intensity of her emotion. "It's our problem, too."

Jenny could feel herself flushing more deeply as a wave of guilt swept her. They didn't understand—they didn't know that she'd almost surrendered of her own free will.

"He's evil," Tom was saying. "You can't just give up and let evil win because of us. You *can't*, Jenny."

Zach's dry voice cut through the impassioned atmosphere. "I don't think," he said, "that there's much point in arguing about it. Because from what Jenny said before, it sounded like she agreed to the new Game."

"I did," Jenny said. "I didn't know—when I agreed I thought he'd leave the rest of you alone. I didn't think you'd be involved."

"And he said the Game had started. Which means—"

"There's nothing she can do to change it now, even if she wanted to." Audrey finished Zach's sentence crisply.

"Like I said"—Dee gave her most bloodthirsty smile—"I think we'd better figure out the rules."

They all looked at one another. Jenny saw the consensus in all their faces. They were all together now, even Tom. Like the old days. All for one and one for all.

She sat down on the love seat beside Tom.

"So what do we need to do to win?" Audrey asked.

"Avoid getting caught," Zach said tersely.

Michael, rummaging glumly in his Cracker Jack, said, *"How?* We can't stay here forever."

"It's not as simple as that," Dee said. "Look—

there are different kinds of games, right? The first Game, the one in the paper house, was like a race game. In a race game the point is to get from the start to the goal in a certain amount of time—or before everybody else does."

"Like Parcheesi," Jenny said.

"No, like Chutes and Ladders!" Michael said, looking up excitedly. "Remember that? You throw the dice and go across the board—and sometimes you can go up a ladder, the way we went up the stairs in the paper house. And sometimes you fall down a chute—"

"—which we did, on the third floor," Dee said.

"We had that game as kids," Zach said with a half glance at Jenny. "Only ours was called *Snakes* and Ladders."

"Okay, the point is that lots of games are race games," Dee went on. She jumped up and began to pace the room. "But then there are hunting games, too—those are actually the oldest games of all. Like hide-and-seek. That started out as practice for stalking wild animals."

"How do you know?" Michael said suspiciously.

"Aba told me. And tag is like capturing domestic animals. This new game Julian is playing is a hunting and capturing game."

Tom shrugged bleakly. "So he's planning to hunt down and capture each of us animals."

"Trophies," Zach said in a low voice. "Like my father's."

"Not like your father's," Dee said, stopping to look at him. "Your father's are dead. This is more like a game where you catch each of the animals and put them in a big pen to wait for the slaughter."

Michael choked on his Coke.

"Well, it's true," Dee said. "He didn't say he was going to kill us one by one. He said he was going to capture us—until the free ones find his base."

Wiping his mouth, Michael said hoarsely, "Let's find it now and avoid the whole thing."

"But that's the *point*," Dee said, sitting on the windowsill. "How do we find it?"

"How *can* we?" Zach said. "It's hopeless."

Tom was still looking into the distance. "There might be another way," he began, and then stopped and shook his head. Jenny didn't like the expression on his face. She didn't like the way the green flecks in his eyes showed.

"Tom . . ." she said, but Audrey was talking to her.

"Didn't he tell you anything about it, Jenny? His base?"

"No," Jenny said. "Only that it was somewhere to keep us before he takes us to the Shadow World."

"Which means it's not in the Shadow World itself," Dee said, and Michael muttered, "Thank God."

"But wherever it is, you get there through the holes?" Audrey said. "Oh, wonderful. I'll pass, thank you."

"These holes, now," Michael said thoughtfully. "I think they're very interesting."

"Maybe because you have one for a brain," Audrey said with a snappishness she hadn't shown to Michael in weeks.

Michael gave her a startled glance quite different from his standard wounded look. "No, really," he said. "You know, they make me think of something.

127

There's a story by Ambrose Bierce—the book's probably around here somewhere." He twisted his head toward the wall-to-wall bookcases that were the main feature of the living room. Michael's father wrote science fiction, and the apartment was filled with strange things. Models of spaceships, posters of obscure SF movies, weird masks—but mainly books. Books overflowing the shelves and lying in piles on the floor. As usual, Michael couldn't find the one he was looking for.

"Well, anyway," he said, "Ambrose Bierce wrote this trilogy about weird disappearances, and there was this one story about a sixteen-year-old boy. His name was Charles Ashmore, and one night after it snowed he went out to the spring to get water. Well, the thing was, he went out the door and he never came back. Afterward, his family went outside to see what was the matter, and they saw his tracks in the snow—and the tracks went halfway to the spring and just stopped dead." Michael lowered his voice dramatically. "Nobody ever saw him again."

"Great," Jenny said. "But what has that got to do with things?"

"Well, the story was *supposed* to be fiction, right? But there was another part in the book, where this German doctor—Dr. Hern, or something—had a theory about how people disappeared. He said that 'in the visible world there are void places'—sort of like the holes in Swiss cheese."

"And that guy fell into one?" Dee said, looking intrigued.

"Fell—or was dragged. Like I said, the stories

were *supposed* to be fiction. But what if there really are voids like that? And what if Julian can—well, control them?"

"That's a nasty idea," Dee said. "I like it."

"Are you saying all people who disappear fall into the Shadow World?" Audrey asked.

"Maybe not all of them, but maybe some of them. And maybe not all the way in, maybe just partway. In the story, when Charles Ashmore's mother went by the place where he disappeared the next day, she could hear his voice. She heard it fainter and fainter every day, until it finally just faded completely."

"A halfway place," Jenny whispered. "Like the More Games store—some place halfway between the Shadow World and here."

Dee was looking at her shrewdly. "Like Julian's base, huh? Somewhere to keep us until he takes us to the Shadow World."

"And you hear about vortex things in Stonehenge and Sedona, Arizona," Michael said. "Was it like a vortex, Audrey?"

"It was big and black," Audrey said shortly. "I don't know how much more vortexy you can get." But she gave Michael the prize from her Cracker Jack, a blue plastic magnifying glass. He put it beside his prize, a mini baseball card.

Jenny was playing absently at her own prize package, not really seeing it. "But it doesn't help us find the base," she said. "Unless we jump into one of those voids, and then I don't think we're coming back."

"It closed up completely," Tom said. "After the

wolf jumped into it, it just disappeared. I don't even think I could find the place again."

"Anyway, I'll bet he can move them around," Michael was beginning, when Jenny gasped.

She had torn open her prize package. She'd been fiddling with the prize, completely preoccupied with the question of voids—until something caught her eye.

"What is it?" Dee said, jumping up from the windowsill.

"It's a book of poetry—or something." It was a very small book, on cheap paper with large print. One sentence per page. But it was a very strange poem for a Cracker Jack prize.

Jenny read:

"In the midst of the word she was trying to say,
In the midst of her laughter and glee,
She had softly and suddenly vanished away—
For the Snark *was* a Boojum, you see."

There was dead silence in the room.

"It could be a coincidence," Zach said slowly.

Michael was shaking his rumpled head. "But those lines are wrong. That's not the way they go—look, *that* book I know I've got." He went into his bedroom and came out with *Alice in Wonderland and Other Favorites*. "They're from a poem about these guys who go out hunting imaginary animals— Snarks. Only some of the Snarks are Boojums, and those hunt *you*. And in the end one of them finds a Snark, and it turns out to be a Boojum. But it's *he* in the poem—'In the midst of the word *he* was trying to say,/ In the midst of *his* laughter and glee . . .' You see?"

"Cracker Jack wouldn't make a mistake like that," Tom said, with a wry smile.

"No," Jenny whispered. "It's from Julian. But is it about what almost happened tonight—or about something that's *going* to happen?"

The silence stretched. Tom's brows were drawn together. Dee had her jaguar look on and was pacing again. Zachary's gray eyes were narrow, his lean body tense and still.

Michael had put down the book. "You think he's giving us clues in advance?"

"It would be—sporting, I guess," Jenny said. "And he gave me a kind of clue on the balcony, remember. He said he'd go after 'Little Red Riding-Hood' first."

Everyone looked at everyone else speculatively. Suddenly Dee whirled and did a swift, flowing punch-and-kick. "Then we might just have a chance!"

Excitement was passing from one of them to another like sparks traveling down a fuse.

"If we can figure the clues out beforehand—and then just *surround* the person they're about . . ." Dee said.

"I know we can! I always wanted to be Sherlock Holmes," said Michael.

"I think it might actually work," Tom said. A new light had kindled in his hazel eyes.

Dee laughed exultantly. "Of course it will work! We're going to beat him."

Jenny was caught up in the fervor herself. Maybe

131

they *could* outthink Julian. "It's not going to be easy—"

"But we'll do it," Audrey said. "Because we have to." She gave Jenny a spiky-lashed glance and picked up several empty Coke cans to take to the kitchen.

"We'd better start with the one we have, then," Zach said, turning a cool, analytical gaze on Jenny's riddle book.

"Unless that one's already finished," Michael said. "I mean, if it was about Audrey—or should I call you Little Red Riding-Hood?" he shouted to the kitchen.

"Call me madam," Audrey said from around the corner, her good humor clearly restored. "Call me Al." She began to sing a Paul Simon song. " 'I can call you Betty, and Betty, when you call me, you can call me—' "

"Well?" Michael yelled when she didn't finish. "What can I call you?"

Audrey didn't answer, and Michael snorted, "Women!"

Zach was saying, "Yeah, but what if it's a new clue? It says *she,* so it's got to be either—"

Jenny heard him as if from a distance. She was listening, listening, and all at once she couldn't breathe.

"Audrey?" she said. The sound of rattling cans in the kitchen had stopped. "Audrey? *Audrey?*"

Everyone was looking at her, frightened by something in her voice. The sound of raw panic, Jenny guessed. Jenny stared back at them, and their images seemed to waver. Utter silence came from the kitchen.

Then she was on her feet and moving. She reached the corner before any of them, even Dee. She looked into the kitchen.

Her screams rang off the light fixture in the ceiling. *"No! No! Oh, God, no!"*

11

The kitchen was empty. A trickle of water ran out of the faucet, and there was an odd, sharp smell. Sitting grotesquely in the middle of the green linoleum floor was a paper doll.

It was folded to allow it to sit, and one arm was twisted up to give it a mockingly casual air. As if Audrey were saying: "Here I am. Where have *you* been?" It was obscene.

Tom's hands were on Jenny's shoulders, trying to calm her. She wrenched away from him and picked the macabre little figure up. It was the doll Audrey had used in the Game, her playing piece in the paper house. Audrey herself had drawn the face, had colored in the hair and clothes with Joey's crayons. Jenny hadn't seen it since she'd packed it up with the rest of the Game in the white box. She realized suddenly that it hadn't been in Angela's toolshed. None of the dolls had.

The waxy face looked up at Jenny with a terrible cunning smile. A *U* of bright pink. As if this doll knew what had happened to the real Audrey, and was glad about it.

"Oh, God—God," Jenny was gasping, almost sobbing. The doll crumpled in her hand. Everything in the kitchen was wavering.

"I don't believe it," Michael said, pushing past the others. "Where is she?" He stared at Jenny, grabbed her arm. "Where is she?"

Tom grabbed Michael. "Let go of her."

"Where's Audrey?"

"I said, let go of her!"

Dee's voice rang out dangerously. "Cool off, both of you!"

"But how did she get out of the kitchen?" Michael said wildly. "We were right around the corner—we didn't hear anything. Nothing could have happened to her. We were right there."

Dee was kneeling on the floor, running her fingers across the linoleum.

"It's darker here—see? This whole area is darker. And it smells burned."

Jenny could see it now, a circle of darker green several feet in diameter.

Tom was still gripping Michael, but his voice was quiet. "You didn't see that thing on the beach—that void, Mike. It didn't make any noise at all. That's how she got out of the kitchen."

" 'In the midst of the word she was trying to say,/ In the midst of her laughter and glee,' " Zachary quoted, behind them.

Jenny turned sharply to see him standing there.

With his thin, intense face and his dark-circled eyes, he looked like a prophet of doom. But when his gray eyes met Jenny's, she knew he cared. He was still holding the poem.

The last of the cloudiness in Jenny's head vanished. Tears and hysterics weren't going to help Audrey. They weren't going to help anyone. She looked down at the crumpled paper doll in her hand.

It was her fault. Audrey had fallen into a black hole, and it was Jenny's fault, just as Summer's death had been. But Audrey wasn't dead yet.

"I'll find her," Jenny said softly to the paper thing she held. "I'll find her, and then I'll rip you to pieces. I'm going to win this Game."

It went on smiling its cunning waxy smile, bland and malevolent.

Michael was sniffling and rubbing his nose. Dee was investigating the floor like an ebony huntress.

"It's like the marks a UFO might leave," she said. "When it lands, I mean. A perfect circle."

"Or a fairy ring," Michael said thickly. "She was so scared of that kind of stuff—legend stuff, you know?" Tom patted him on the back.

"The Erlking," Jenny said grimly. She reached across Tom to grip the sleeve of Michael's sweatshirt. "But we got her back from him last time, Michael. We'll get here back now."

Dee stood in one fluid, graceful motion. "I think we'd all better stay together from now on," she said.

Zach had moved up behind Jenny. The five of them *were* together, standing in one connected knot in the center of the kitchen. Jenny felt herself draw strength from all the others.

"We can sleep in the living room," Michael said. "On the floor. We can push the furniture back."

They raided the bedrooms for blankets and mattresses and found sleeping bags in the closet. In the bathroom Jenny stripped off her golden dress and put on an old sweatsuit of Michael's. She jammed the shimmering material in the laundry hamper, never wanting to see it again.

It scared her to be alone even for a minute.

But we haven't had another clue, she thought. He can't do anything else without another clue. It wouldn't be fair.

"It wouldn't be *sporting*," she said through her teeth to the wall. It had suddenly occurred to her that Julian might be able to hear her. To see her, even— he'd watched her from the shadows for years. It was a disturbing thought, to know that no place was private, but right now Jenny hoped he was listening.

"It's no Game at all if we don't have a chance," she told the wall softly but fiercely.

In the living room she sat down on a mattress next to Tom. He put an arm around her, and she rested against him, glad of his warmth and solidity.

If there was one tiny comfort in all of this, it was that Tom was with her again. She snuggled into his arm and shut her eyes. This was where she could forget about Julian—forget about everything dark and terrible. Tom's strong warm hand clasped hers, held tightly.

Then she felt the pressure released and sensed the change in Tom's body. Tension flooding in. He was holding her hand up, looking at it.

No, not at her hand. At the ring.

The golden band which had felt like ice on her finger earlier that night had warmed to her body temperature. She hadn't even noticed it for hours.

Now, horrified, she snatched her hand back from Tom's. She tried to pull the ring off. It wouldn't come.

Soap, she thought. She pulled frantically, twisting the circlet, reddening her finger. Soap or butter or—

It was no good.

She knew without even trying. The ring was on to stay. She could do anything she liked, but it wouldn't come off until Julian wanted it to. If she could have gotten it off, she might have been able to change the words inside—and Julian would never risk that. He'd said that speaking and writing words made them true. He would never take the chance that Jenny might change the words and change her fate.

"We're going to win the Game," she said to the shuttered darkness in Tom's eyes. "When we win, I'm free of my promise." She said it almost pleadingly—but Tom's face remained closed. He'd gone away again, leaving a polite stranger in his place.

"We'd better get to sleep," he said and turned to his own pile of blankets.

Jenny was left sitting there, feeling the inscription on the inside of the ring as if the letters were burning their way into her skin.

Nothing is as frightening as waking up and not knowing who you are, not knowing it's *you* waking. It happened to Jenny Sunday morning. She opened her eyes and didn't know which direction was which.

She didn't know her place in the world, where she was in time and space.

Then she remembered. Michael's living room. They were there because of Julian.

She sat up so suddenly that it made her dizzy, and she frantically looked for the others.

They were all there. Michael was curled almost in a ball under his blanket; Dee was sprawled lazily on the couch like a sleeping lioness. Zach was on his back on the floor, his blond ponytail streaming on his pillow. Tom was beside him, face turned toward Jenny, one hand stretched toward her. As if he'd reached out in his sleep, unaware of it.

Jenny took a moment to look at him. He looked different asleep, very young and vulnerable. At times she loved him so much it was like a physical ache, a pain in her chest.

Dee yawned and stretched, sitting up. "Everybody here?" she said, instantly alert and oriented. "Then let's kick Michael and make him get us some breakfast. We're guests."

Tom pulled his hand away when he woke up, and avoided Jenny's eyes.

"Do you really think we can get away with it?" Michael asked doubtfully.

"We've got to," Jenny said. "What else are we going to say to them? 'I'm sorry; your daughter's been kidnapped, but don't worry because we're going to get her back'?"

"It'll be all right as long as we get the housekeeper," Dee said. "I'll talk to her while you go upstairs."

"Then we'll go by your place," Jenny said, "and

you can tell your parents you're staying with me. And Zach can tell his parents he's staying with Tom, and Tom—"

"But the question is: will they buy it?" Michael said. "I mean, we're not talking about just one night, here. It could be days before we find that base."

"We'll tell them we've got a school project," Jenny said, "and it may take a few nights of working on it. We'll *make* them buy it. We have to."

She and Dee and Zach went in Dee's jeep, while Tom and Michael followed in the RX-7. Tom hadn't said a word to her all morning, and Jenny tried to hide her left hand whenever she could. She felt as if the ring were a badge of shame.

They'd decided to go everywhere together from now on. Nobody was ever to be alone, and whenever possible all five of them were to be in the same place. They pulled up in tandem to Audrey's house, and Dee and Jenny knocked on the door while the boys watched from the sidewalk.

"Hi, Gabrielle," Dee said to the housekeeper who answered. "Are Mr. and Mrs. Myers here? Oh, too bad. Well, could you tell them that Audrey's going to spend a couple nights with Jenny and me at Jenny's?"

Meanwhile, Jenny speedily headed up the stairs of the stately house and came back a few minutes later with an armful of clothes. "Audrey just asked me to pick up a few things for her," she said brightly to Gabrielle, and then she and Dee made a fast retreat.

"Whew!" Dee said when they were back in the jeep. Jenny blinked away tears. Handling Audrey's clothes had brought the sense of guilt back. But it had to be done. Audrey would never go anywhere overnight without a few different outfits.

"We probably should have taken her car," Dee said. "She takes *that* everywhere, too."

"Maybe later," said Jenny. "I picked up her keys while I was in her bedroom."

"Next victim," Zachary said from the back seat.

Tom disposed of his parents quickly; he and Michael came out of his Spanish-style house with a bundle of clothes each.

"And a few textbooks," Michael said. "For authenticity."

Jenny's mother was at church. Jenny shouted her message to her father, who was bent over the pool, wrestling with the floating cleaner. "Gonna stay with Dee for a few days, Dad! We're working on a big physiology project!"

"Call us occasionally to let us know you're alive," her father said, pushing his glasses up by hunching his shoulder and not releasing his grip on the pool cleaner.

Jenny gave him one quick frightened glance before she realized it was a joke. Mr. Thornton complained a lot about being the father of a teenager with an active social schedule. She surprised him by running up and kissing his sweaty cheek.

"I will, Daddy. I love you." Then she ran away again.

It was at Zach's house that they ran into trouble.

They were giddy with their previous successes, and not prepared when they pulled up to the mock Tudor house on Quail Run. Jenny went into the garage with Zach while the others talked to Jenny's aunt Lily.

"You keep your textbooks out here?"

"The art ones. And I figure we might as well bring a flashlight." He took one off a hook on the wall.

Jenny looked around the studio Zach had made in the garage. Being here made her think about Julian, about the time in the paper house when he had impersonated Zach. Flustered, she stared at a print on the wall. It was a giant mural print showing school cafeteria tables stacked in a glorious pyramid, four high and four deep, almost blocking the exit. Zach had taken it last year after she and Tom and Dee and he had stacked the tables one night. They'd left the tables that way for the VGHS staff to find the next morning.

Jenny tried to concentrate on the fun of that night, her mind adding color to the gray tones of the picture, but a soft assault on all her senses had begun. She kept seeing Zach's face in her mind, watching it turn to Julian's. Feeling the softness of Julian's hair under her fingers.

"You okay, Jenny? You look kind of red."

"Oh, no, no, I'm fine." More flustered than ever, she added hastily, "So what have you done lately? You haven't shown me any new prints for a while."

Zach's shoulders hunched slightly, and he looked away. "I've been busy with other things," he said.

Jenny blinked. That was a new one. Zach too busy for his photos? But she had to make conversation; she was afraid to let the silence go on.

"What's this?" she said, touching a textbook that lay open on the desk.

"Magritte," Zach said succinctly.

"Magritte? He was a painter, right?"

"A Belgian surrealist." Suddenly focused, Zach

picked up the textbook. He looked at it almost fiercely, his features sharp. "Look at this," he said, opening it to a new page. "I was thinking about doing something that would catch the same mood. I just wish . . ." His voice trailed off.

Jenny looked and saw an extremely weird picture. It showed a brown pipe, the kind Audrey's father smoked, with the words *This is not a pipe* under it.

Jenny stared at it, feeling stupid. Beside her, Zach was tense, waiting for her response.

"But—it is a pipe," she said timidly, tapping her finger on the brown bowl.

Zach's gray eyes were still on the book. "No, it isn't."

"Yes, it is."

"No, it isn't. A picture of a pipe is not a pipe."

For a moment she got it—then it slipped away. It made her head hurt, but it also gave her a vaguely excited feeling. Mystical.

"The image isn't reality," Zach said quietly but with force. "Even though we're used to thinking that way a lot of the time. We show a kid a picture of a dog and say 'This is a doggie'—but it's *not*. It's just an image." He glanced at her sideways and added, "A paper house is not a house."

"Unless you have somebody who can *make* an image into reality," Jenny said, giving him a meaningful glance back.

"Maybe he's an artist, in a way," Zach said. He flipped to another page. "See this? It's a famous painting."

It was another extremely weird picture, but it took you a moment to see the weirdness. It showed a window in a room, and through the window a pretty

143

landscape. Hills and trees and clouds. Only—it was odd, but under the window were three metal things like the legs of a stand. The legs of an easel, Jenny realized suddenly. There was actually an easel with a canvas on it in front of the window, but the painting on the canvas blended in so exactly with the landscape behind it that it was almost invisible.

It left you wondering: Where was the artist who had left the easel? And who could have painted a picture that blended in so exactly with reality, anyway?

"It's bizarre," Jenny said. "I like it." She smiled at Zach, feeling as if they had a secret. She saw his expression change, and then he looked away, his gray eyes distant.

"It's important to know the difference between image and reality," he said softly. He glanced at her sideways again, as if considering whether to tell her another secret. Considering whether she could be trusted. Then he said almost casually, "You know, I used to think that imaginary worlds were safer than the real one. Then I saw a *real* imaginary world. And it was—" He stopped.

Jenny was startled at his expression. She put her hand on his arm. "I know."

He looked at her. "Remember how we used to play in the orchard when we were kids? It didn't seem important then to know the difference between what's real and what isn't. But it's important now. It's important to me."

Oh. All at once, Jenny understood. No wonder Zach had been so moody lately. His photography, his art—it wasn't safe anymore. It had been contaminated by their experience in the Shadow World. For the first time in his life Zach was having to face squarely up to reality.

"That's why you haven't done any new prints," she said. "Isn't it, Zach? It's—it's artist's block."

He hunched one shoulder again. "I just haven't seen anything I wanted to photograph. I used to see things all the time and want to shoot them—but lately I just don't care."

"I'm sorry, Zach." But I'm glad you told me, Jenny thought. She felt very close to her cousin just then. She went on in a low voice, "Maybe when this is all over—"

She was cut off by the bang of a door. The quiet moment was shattered. Zach's father stood in the doorway.

He said hello briefly to Jenny, then turned to Zach.

"So here you are," he said. "What's this about you taking off without telling anyone last night?"

Jenny had never been sure she liked her uncle Bill. He was a big man, and he had large hairy hands. His face always seemed rather flushed.

Zach's voice was cool and bloodless. "I just went to spend the night somewhere. Is that a crime?"

"It is when you don't tell your mother or me."

"I left a note."

Mr. Taylor's face got more flushed. "I'm not talking about a note. I don't know what's going on with you anymore. You used to spend most of your time holed up out here"—he gestured around the garage—"and now you're gone all the time. Your mother says you think you're going to spend another night away from home."

"I've got a project to do—"

"Then you can do it right here. You're not staying

out overnight on a school night. If you think that, you've got another think coming."

Jenny's stomach had a falling-elevator feeling. She opened her mouth, trying to think of something, anything to say. But she could see by her uncle's face that it wouldn't do any good. He was as stubborn as Zach; stubborner.

The door banged again as he left.

Jenny whirled in dismay. "What are we going to do?"

"Nothing." Face turned from her, Zach slapped the art book shut and put it back on the pressed-wood shelf.

"But, Zach, we have to—"

"Look, if you argue with him, he'll just get madder —and he might start calling around. Do you want him to talk to *your* parents?" He turned back, and his thin face was calm, although Jenny thought his eyes looked a little sore. "Don't rock the boat, Jenny. Maybe he'll let me come tomorrow."

"But for tonight—"

"I'll be okay. You just—just watch out for yourself, all right?" He moved when Jenny tried to put a hand on his arm and added, "Tell everybody else what happened, will you? I think I'll just stay here a while. Do some work."

Jenny's hand dropped. "Okay, Zach," she said softly. She blinked. "Goodbye. I mean—see you later." She turned and went quickly out of the garage.

"Now what?" Dee said when they were back at the apartment. They were all quiet, their triumph deflated.

146

"Now we order some pizza and wait," Michael said.

"And *think*," Jenny said. "We have to figure out where that base is."

Jenny woke up with a start and thought, hypnopompic hallucination? I think I'm awake, but I'm still dreaming.

Julian was leaning over her.

"Tom!" she cried, turning to see him lying on the floor beside her, his breathing deep and even. Her cry didn't wake him.

"Don't bother. It's only a dream. Come in the other room, where we can have a little privacy."

Jenny, who was wearing her own sweatsuit tonight instead of Michael's, pulled her blanket up higher. Like some Victorian girl in a lacy nightgown. "You're crazy," she told him with dream-calmness. "If I go in there, you'll kidnap me."

"I won't. I promise." His teeth gleamed at her briefly, wolflike. "Remember Perthro?"

The rune of gambling, Jenny thought, seeing in her mind's eye the lines he'd sketched in the air on the night of the prom. The rune of fair play, of sticking to the rules. Meaning he kept his promises, she supposed. Or that he would keep this one. Or that he *said* he would.

But he might give me a clue about the base, Jenny thought. She and the others hadn't had much luck figuring it out for themselves. And it was a dream, anyway. She got up and followed him to Michael's bedroom, where the clock radio said 4:33 A.M.

"Where's Audrey?" she demanded as he turned to face her. If this had been reality, she would have been frightened of him, maybe too frightened to speak. But it was a dream, and everything she did was governed by dream-logic.

"Safe."

"But where *is* she?"

"That would be telling." His eyes swept over her and he smiled. "I have to say it; you look equally good in grunge and high fashion."

It wasn't a dream. The way he disturbed and excited Jenny was too real. By Michael's bedside lamp she could see his eyes, which at the prom had been shadowed by his mask. She had finally figured out what color they were. It was the blue you see when you're washing your face in the shower and your fingers press on your closed lids. You see filaments of brightness etched against the black, more vibrant than electric blue. A color that isn't really in the wavelengths of light that the human eye can perceive. The color Jenny had seen in afterimage when the computer flashed.

Jenny looked away, simultaneously holding out her hand to him. "I want this off, please. Just until the Game is over, take the ring off."

He took her hand instead, stroking her palm with his thumb. "Is it making Tommy nervous?"

"No—I don't know. I don't like it." She looked at him again, trying to pull her hand away. His fingers were cooler than Tom's, but just as strong. "I *hate* you, you know," she said earnestly. She couldn't see why he never seemed to understand this. "You make me hate you."

"Is that what you're feeling? Hate?"

Jenny was trembling. Stubbornly she nodded.

Very gently he reeled her in by the captive hand, drawing her to him. She'd been wrong. He wasn't as strong as Tom; he was stronger. Fight or scream? Jenny thought. But he was so close now. She could feel the movement of his breathing. Her heart was beating in the base of her throat.

She could feel her eyes widen as she looked up at him. His expression made her stomach flutter. "What are you going to do?"

"I'm going to kiss you . . ."

Oh, was that all?

". . . until you faint."

Then shadows seemed to fill all the corners of the room and close in about her.

But some part of her mind still had strength. She didn't faint, although her legs went weak again. She pushed him away.

"You're *evil*," she whispered. "How do you think I could ever love something evil? Unless I'm evil, too. . . ."

She was beginning to wonder about this. But he laughed. "There is no good and evil, only black and white. But either black or white on its own is boring, Jenny. If you mix them you get so many colors—so many colors. . . ."

She turned away. She heard him pick something up, one of Michael's books.

"Here," he said. "Have you read this one?"

It was a poem, "The Human Condition" by Howard Nemerov. Jenny's eyes skimmed over it, not really understanding any of it. It muddled her.

"It's about world and thought," Julian explained. "World being the world, you see, and thought being

—everything else. Image. As opposed to reality." He smiled at her. "That's a hint, incidentally."

Jenny was still muddled. She couldn't seem to focus on the poem, and she was strangely tired. Like the old hypnotist's saying, her eyes were heavy. Her whole body felt warm and heavy.

Julian put his arms around her, supporting her. "You'd better wake up now."

"You mean I'd better go to sleep."

"I mean wake up. If you don't want to be late." She felt his lips on her forehead and realized her eyes were shut.

She had to open them . . . she had to open her eyes . . . But she was drifting, somewhere dark and silent and warm. Just drifting . . . floating . . .

Some time later Jenny forced her eyes open. Blinked. She was lying on Michael's living room floor.

It had been a dream after all.

But beside her was an open book, facedown. *Contemporary Poetry*. Jenny picked it up and saw the poem Julian had shown her.

Now that she was awake and thinking clearly, the poem made more sense; it was even vaguely exciting. But she didn't have time to appreciate it; her eye fixed on certain words and her heart began to pound.

Once I saw world and thought exactly meet,
But only in a picture by Magritte. . . .

The poem went on about the picture of a picture by Magritte—the one Zach had shown Jenny. The one of a painting that stood in front of an open window, matching the landscape outside exactly.

Fitting in like a puzzle piece, standing alone in an empty room.

Magritte, Jenny thought. Oh, God! *An empty room.*

Dropping the book, she seized Tom's shoulder. "Tom! Tom, get up! Dee! Michael! It's Zach!"

12

Zach was asleep when he first felt the creeping around his legs. Or half asleep, anyway—he hadn't really slept for days now. He hadn't dreamed. His daytime thoughts went on going even when he lay there with his eyes shut for hours.

He'd wondered what happened to you when you didn't dream for days. Hallucinations while you were walking around?

Tonight, though, he was definitely drifting when he felt the touch on his ankle. A smooth, rubbery feeling. For a moment he was paralyzed, and a moment was all it took. The rubbery feeling wound its way up his leg, his stomach, his chest. It tightened like a living rope, cutting off his breathing.

Zach's eyes flew open, and he saw clearly the head of the snake staring into his face. Its eyes were two dots of shining light; its mouth was open so wide it looked as if its jaw were dislocated. As if it were going to *eat* him. Out of that gaping mouth came an endless menacing *hisssssssss*. . . .

Unable to move, Zach stared up at the swaying shape. Then, somehow, his perspective changed. His eyes ached from staring, but he couldn't see the snake's head anymore. The two dots of light looked more like two of the glow-in-the-dark stars he'd stuck on his ceiling when he was eight—he'd scraped most of them off when his father yelled, but a few remained.

He couldn't hear the hiss now, either. Only the *shhshhshhshh* of the air-conditioning.

His arms and legs were tangled up in the bedclothes.

God, he thought, and kicked the sheet and blanket off. He got up and turned on the light. Now he knew what happened when you went for days without dreaming. Of course there was no snake in his bed.

The last thing he wanted to do was lie down again, though. Might as well go out to the garage. Even if he couldn't work, it might take his mind off things.

When he got to the garage, the snake was waiting for him.

It wasn't like a real snake. It was a surrealist painter's idea of a snake—swirls of darkness that bunched and surged in a snakelike motion. Blue-white light connecting murky segments of body. A sort of combination between a snake and a lightning bolt in a storm.

It came toward him with the blind hunching of a tomato worm. It was at least ten feet long.

If I could get it over into the corner, Zach thought, his mind cold and clear . . . He glanced at the corner of the garage where his 6x6 SLR stood on a tripod. If he could get it over there, he was almost sure he could get a picture of it.

He wasn't stupid. He saw the danger he was in. But the idea of photographing this thing—seeing what it would look like on film—drove every other thought out of his mind.

It was the first time he'd cared about getting a picture since the day of the Game. All at once his artist's block disappeared, his creativity came rushing back. This was *real* unreality. It might be unsafe, but it was strangely beautiful, too. It was Art.

He was desperate to capture it.

Try the 35 millimeter first, his mind told him. It's closer. Eyes fixed on the wonderfully artistic monster, he reached for the camera on the desk.

The clock in Dee's jeep said 5:45. More than an hour later than it had been in Jenny's dream of Michael's room.

"Oh, God, we're going to be too late," she whispered.

And it was her fault. She hadn't woken up in time. Even with Julian's warning, she hadn't woken up in time.

"Hurry up, Dee! Hurry!"

Trees were silhouetted against a flamingo dawn when they reached Zach's house.

"Let's go through the garage," Tom said as they all jumped out of the jeep. "Last time I was here, the door was unlocked."

Zach wouldn't be so stupid tonight, Jenny thought, but there was no time to argue. She was following the others at a run to the side door of the garage. The door opened under Tom's hand, and they all burst inside.

The garage light was on. There was a sharp, strange smell to the air. A dark circle of soot on the floor.

In its center was a paper doll with gray eyes.

"I was too late," Jenny said stupidly, looking down at the paper-doll Zach she was holding. It stared back at her, the fine lines of its face shaded by Zach's artist's hand. The penciled eyes seemed vaguely surprised.

Dee was rubbing the soot between her fingers. Tom was standing in front of the corner where Zach's camera and a tungsten floodlamp lay knocked over.

"There was a fight," he said.

Michael just licked his lips and shivered.

"His parents must not have heard anything," Jenny said slowly, after a moment. "Or they'd be down here. So we'd better write them a note—from Zach, saying that he's gone to school already."

Michael's voice was subdued. "You're crazy. We can't keep this up. Eventually some of your parents are going to *talk* to each other—"

"What good is it going to do my aunt and uncle to know Zach's gone? What can they do?"

"Put us in orange coveralls," Dee said from the floor. "Too many disappearances," she added succinctly. "If we lose any more friends, we're going to jail. Now, come on, stop talking, and let's get out of here."

Jenny crept into the house and wrote the note before they left.

Back in the car Tom said, "I don't see how *we* can go to school ourselves. Not and stick together."

"Then we'll have to take the day off," Dee said. "Gosh, too bad."

Michael looked at her balefully from the front passenger seat. "You're enjoying this, aren't you?"

She gave him a distinctly uncivilized smile.

"We've *got* to figure out where the base is," Jenny was saying in the back seat. She'd controlled herself very well this time, she thought: no screaming or crying even when she saw the paper doll of Zach. But the rasping feeling of guilt was still with her. "I haven't been very good at figuring out the clues so far," she said, keeping her voice level so the others wouldn't think she was drowning in self-pity.

"Because Julian *wants* it that way," Dee said. Jenny had told them about the dream—leaving out the kiss—on the drive to Zach's house. "He's not playing this Game straight. We got the first clue in plenty of time, but it was too hard. The second clue was dead easy, but there wasn't time to do anything about it."

"I should have woken up sooner," Jenny said in a low voice.

Beside her, Tom started to reach for her, and Jenny saw his face, all planes and shadows in the early morning light. Tom Locke even looked good at the crack of dawn; he woke up looking that way.

Tom's hand dropped back to his side. Jenny knew what it was without asking. She was sitting on his right in the car, and her left hand, with the ring, was in between them.

She looked out the window fiercely and pretended she didn't mind.

"You know, there's one reason I did want to go to

156

school today," she said. "To try and find out about Eric—the guy Audrey was with. See if he's okay."

"I could probably call his house and ask. I know him a little," Tom said, to show he was still talking to her, even if he wouldn't touch her. Oh, we're terribly courteous, Jenny thought. For all the good that does.

"We can call from the apartment," Michael said. "We should probably get some food first."

"No, I tell you what let's do," Dee said, her voice excited. "Let's go see Aba."

"This early?"

"Not everybody sleeps like you, Mikey. Besides, she'll give us breakfast."

In the back seat Jenny leaned forward. A heavy weight seemed to have lifted from her chest, at least for the moment. "You're right," she said to Dee. "Let's go see Aba. Maybe she knows what we should do."

Aba lived in a house beside Dee's mother's house. The two buildings were on the same property, but Aba's house had a distinctly different character. Dee and her friends always called it the Art Pavilion.

One entire wing was devoted to Aba's craft, centering around the studio where she did her sculpting. The large, airy room was all soaring asymmetrical walls and skylights.

Aba was at work when the children came in, taking moist gray clay from a bowl and slapping it on a wire armature.

"What's it going to be?" Dee asked, coming up behind her.

"Good morning," Aba said firmly, and when they'd all said good morning, she said, "A bust of

Neetu Badhu, your mother's manicurist. She has a very interesting face, and she's due here at seven."

"Then we'd better hurry," Dee said. "Is it okay if we use your phone? And get some breakfast?"

"There are caramel rolls in the kitchen," Aba said. "Get them—and then come back and tell me why you're here."

While the others went to the kitchen, Tom got on the phone.

"Eric's okay," he said when he hung up. "He was home from school today, but there's nothing really wrong with him. The police are interested in talking with anybody who saw the attack, though—which means Audrey."

Michael stopped eating his roll. "Which means they might be trying to track her down," he said. "Great."

"Don't worry about it, Mikey," Dee said comfortingly. "You'll probably be next, so you won't be here when our Great Deception comes crashing down."

"Dee," Aba said, "have you been telling lies?"

"Yup. Our whole life these last few days has been a tissue of fibs."

Aba shook her head and wiped her clay-smeared hands on her denim smock. "Now," she said to the group, "tell me."

And they did. They told her the truth about what had been happening since they'd been released from the police station; how they'd been looking for the paper house, how they'd found it, what Julian had said to Jenny about the new Game. And what had happened to Zach and Audrey.

Aba listened to it all, her beautiful old face grave and attentive. When seven o'clock came, she sent the manicurist away, covered the bust with a wet cloth, and kept listening.

When they finished, she sat quietly for a moment. Jenny half expected her to say something about how wrong it was to deceive their parents—Aba was an adult, after all. She half expected Aba to say that Dee couldn't stay with the rest of them because it was too dangerous. And, although she didn't expect it, she wished passionately that Aba would say, "Here's the answer," and solve all their problems for them.

Aba did none of these things. Instead, after several minutes of quiet sitting, she said, "You know, last night I dreamed a Hausa story my mother used to tell me. It's been a long, long time since I thought of that story. I wonder if I didn't dream it for you."

"For us?"

"Yes. Maybe I was meant to tell it to you." She sat back and thought for a moment, then began, "The story is about a boy and a girl who were in love. But one day, as they were sitting on their mat together, Iblis came along and cut off the boy's head and killed him."

"Iblis?" The name sounded vaguely familiar to Jenny. "Who's that?"

"Iblis," Aba said gravely, "is the prince of darkness, the prince of the *aljunnu*—"

"The genies," Dee said, her eyes flashing at Jenny.

"Yes," Aba said. "But in our folklore the *aljunnu* were not kind genies. They were powerful and evil spirits, and Iblis was their leader. My mother never told me why he cut the boy's head off—but then Iblis always liked to do evil and mischief; maybe he had no particular reason. In any case, Iblis killed the boy, and the girl could do nothing but sit on the mat and cry. After a while the boy's parents came along, and when they saw what had happened, they began to cry, too.

"Then Iblis came back. He waved his hand, and the ground rocked. In front of the boy there appeared a river of fire, a river of water, and a river of cobras. And Iblis turned to the boy's mother and said, "If you would like to bring your son back to life, all you have to do is swim through the three rivers to get him."

"Yeah, right," Michael muttered almost inaudibly. Aba smiled at him and went on.

"But," she said, "the boy's mother was afraid. She turned to her husband, but he was just as frightened.

"Then the girl jumped up. 'I'll do it,' she said. Naturally, she was terribly afraid, but her love for the boy was stronger than her fear. Without another word the girl dived into the river of fire. The fire burned her, of course—my mother always said 'the fire burned her like fire'—but she swam through it and leaped into the river of water. And the water choked her—like water—but the girl struggled through it and fell into the river of snakes. And the snakes struck at her—"

"—like snakes—" Dee put in, grinning.

"—but the girl managed to stumble through them, and the next thing she knew she had reached the boy.

"As soon as she touched him, the boy's head flew to his shoulders and he jumped up, alive and well. Iblis left, cursing, to do his mischief in some other part of the world. And I suppose the boy and the girl got married, although I don't really remember what my mother said about that.

"Well," Aba said, looking around at them. "That's

the story as my mother told it to me. I don't know what meaning it has for you—maybe none. But you've heard it now."

"Maybe it just means that love can be stronger than fear," Jenny said softly.

"Maybe it means you can't trust your parents," Michael said, absolutely deadpan, and Aba laughed.

"I like Jenny's interpretation better. But as I said, there may be no meaning. Or possibly it's just a story about the relative powers of good and evil."

Jenny looked up quickly. "Do you believe in good and evil?"

"Oh, yes. Very strongly. And I believe that evil sometimes has to be fought—personally. Hand to hand. If you care enough to do it."

Michael stirred. "You know what they say about kids our age. That we don't care about right or wrong or anything. That we don't even care about the future."

"Yeah, like the Baby Busters," Dee said, grinning.

"Naw, we're too young even to be Baby Busters. We're the Busted Babies."

Jenny spoke seriously. "It's not *true*. We do care. You care, Michael, more than just about anybody I've ever known. You pretend you don't, but you do. And that's why Audrey loves—" She stopped because Michael was looking away, his sarcastic spaniel eyes filmed over. "We're going to *find* Audrey," she said, her own throat tight.

"I know," Michael said and rubbed at the bridge of his nose with his fingers.

"I wish I could help," Aba said. "But I'm an old woman. My fighting days are over."

"Well, mine aren't," Dee said, raising a slim arm

to examine the hard muscle under velvet skin. "Mine are just starting." Aba looked at her and smiled slightly. For years she and Dee had fought about Dee preferring kung fu to college and insisting that she didn't want to do anything brainy like her mother or arty like her grandmother. But just then Jenny knew Aba was proud of her warrior grand-daughter.

"It's our fight anyway," Jenny said. "He won't let anyone else into the Game. The original players, he said."

"I think," Aba said, looking directly at her, "that if anyone can find your friends, it will be you, Jenny." Her eyes were very gentle and very sad; they reminded Jenny of pictures of Albert Einstein. At that moment Jenny thought that Aba really was *more* beautiful than Dee.

"I'll try," Jenny said. As the old woman turned away, Jenny just caught the murmured words, "But I wonder what the cost will be."

Before they left, Aba let them raid the kitchen. They took cottage cheese and cold chicken breasts; cereal and microwave brownies and grapes and pippin apples.

On the way back they stopped by Audrey's house and picked up Audrey's car.

Michael's living room was beginning to look like the aftermath of a very long party, Jenny thought as they walked into the apartment. The furniture had been pushed to the extreme edges of the room to make room for the mattresses and sleeping bags on the floor. The plaid couch was a nest of rumpled blankets. Empty Coke cans were scattered everywhere, and most flat surfaces were crowded with books or clothes or stacks of dirty dishes.

"Okay," Dee said, coming in from the kitchen with Michael. "Now what about that base?" She sat down on a footstool with a bowl of cottage cheese and chopped apple.

"We don't have enough information," Jenny said. "He hasn't told me enough." Every time she said *he*, Tom walled up. There was no help for it, just as there was no help for the shining thing on her finger. It caught every glint of the spring sunlight coming in Michael's front window, and she swore she could feel the words on the inside of the band.

"I've been trying to think," she said, "about abandoned buildings or things—places around here he might hold them. But that doesn't seem right."

"In mysteries," Michael said thoughtfully, "things are always hidden in the least likely place. Or the most obvious place—because you always think that's the least likely. I guess it couldn't be the paper house."

"It was trashed," Jenny said. "I don't think it would hold anything. Besides, how could we get in on our own? It was Julian who brought us in last time." She knew, somehow, that Julian's base wasn't in the paper house. And she knew something else: Julian wouldn't find the Game amusing unless there was a *chance* of them finding the base. He would put it somewhere they could get to—if they were smart enough to figure out where to look.

"I guess the More Games store is *too* obvious," Michael murmured.

"Too obvious and gone," said Jenny. "It's just a

mural now. No, Julian would put it somewhere *clever.*"

"What is it, Tom?" Dee said. "You have an idea?"

Tom was wearing the look he wore mostly these days—one of abstraction. Just now he also seemed disturbed. He got up and walked toward the kitchen, fingers in his back pockets.

"If you think you know something . . ." Dee said.

"No. Nothing." Tom shook his head and sat back down.

"Okay, let's go back to the beginning," Michael said.

But it didn't help. They talked uselessly through the morning and most of the afternoon, until an elderly woman came and rang the doorbell, demanding that Michael move Audrey's car because it was in her parking space.

Dee went down with him. Tom paced the hallway slowly while Jenny sat on the couch staring aimlessly out the window. They were stuck, no closer to figuring out where the base was than they had been two days ago.

And she was tired. She let her eyelids shut, seeing the golden afternoon sunlight on her closed lids. Then suddenly the light went dark.

Jenny's eyes flew open. Although it had been a bright, cloudless day, there was some sort of mist coating the window. Preventing her from seeing out. Jenny stared at it, pulse quickening, then she drew in her breath and leaned closer.

It wasn't mist—that would have been strange enough. But it was something stranger than that. It was ice.

Touched by the Frost King, Jenny's mother used to say back in Pennsylvania when the windows iced up like that. Jenny hadn't seen it since she was five years old. In those days she'd loved to trace things in the frost with the warmth of her finger. . . .

Something was appearing on the window as if traced by an unseen finger. A letter.

L.

Jenny couldn't breathe. Her mouth opened to call for Tom, but no sound came out.

I. T. T. L. E. . . .

Little. The letters appeared slowly as if a fingertip were tracing them on the icy window.

M. I. S. S. M. U. F. F. E. T. S. A. T. . . .

Jenny watched, scalp crawling. She couldn't seem to make herself move. It was too *strange*, to be sitting here in daylight and seeing something that simply couldn't happen.

O. N. A. T. U. F. F. E. T. E. A. T. I. N. G. H. E. R. . . .

It's me, Jenny thought, gripped by an irrational certainty. This time it's me he's after. I'm Miss Muffet.

C. U. R. D. S. A. N. D. W. H. E. Y. A. L. O. N. G. . . .

Still unable to move, Jenny's eyes shifted upward. A spider. She was afraid of spiders, and crickets, and all crawly, jumpy things. She expected to see a thread descending from the ceiling, but there was nothing.

C. A. M. E. A. S. P. I. D. E. R. A. N. D. S. A. T. D. O. W. N. B. E. S. I. D. E. H. E. R. . . .

The Spider. *The Spider*, Jenny thought. *Audrey's car.*

"Tom," she whispered. And then suddenly she was moving, tearing her eyes from the letters that were still appearing. "Tom, come here. *Tom!*"

As she ran she almost fell over the footstool where Dee had been sitting earlier. Eating cottage cheese, small curd. Curds and whey.

Stupid old lady," Michael said as Dee pulled the Spider out of the carport. "She doesn't even use this space, but will she let anybody else park here? God forbid. Now we have to go all the way down to the garage—take a left up there and go around the trash cans."

"I didn't even know this place had a garage," Dee said.

"Dad and I never use it," Michael said as Dee pulled into a dark entrance and headed down a ramp. "The carports are a lot more convenient."

"Yeah, but right now it's probably a good idea to have Audrey's car down here. In fact, we might want to put *all* the cars here—if somebody notices them outside your apartment, it's a dead giveaway that we're all here. We should have thought of that before."

"I guess," Michael said without enthusiasm. "I dunno—when I was a kid I always hated this place. I had the idea there ought to be a dragon at the bottom of it."

Dee grinned. "It's just a garage, Mikey." But he was right, she thought. There was something unpleasant about the garage. It was dingy and badly lit, and she could see how a kid with an active imagination might think of dragons.

Don't be ridiculous, she told herself. It's broad daylight—but it wasn't. They had turned the corner to the lower level of the garage, and it was as dark as twilight down here with the flickering bluish fluorescents on the ceiling. A strange and unnatural twilight.

Even as she thought it, the lights around them flickered wildly and went out.

It was like being plunged into the tunnel on a roller coaster. Dee suddenly felt that everything was happening too fast—while at the same time it was all happening in slow motion, frame by frame.

Her eyes weren't dark-adapted yet—in that first instant she could see nothing. But she heard the growl from the back of the car clearly.

It was a thick, clotted, animal sound. A *large* sound—the timbre alone let you know that only something big could have produced it. So low and dragging that it sounded like a soundtrack in slow motion. It sounded like a hallucination.

"*What*—" Michael was tearing at his seat belt, turning to look. Dee saw the whites of his eyes. Then, as she twisted her head over her shoulder, she got a glimpse of what was in the back of the car.

Pale eyes and white teeth in gaping jaws. Dee's vision was adapting. She saw a hulking shape materializing in that incredibly small space—as if it were coming through a door in the area between the cabin and the trunk. Coming and coming like a genie emerging from a bottle.

It isn't all the way out yet, Dee realized.

There was no time to think about anything. "Get out!" she shouted. Michael was frozen, clutching the seat and gasping. Dee reached across him, fingers clenching on the Spider's door handle. She flung the door open and shoved him, braking automatically at the same instant.

Michael went tumbling and thudding out. Dee felt a rush of air on her cheek—warm as the blast from under a microwave, and wet. A feral, musky odor made her nostrils flare.

The snarl was directly in her ear.

Move, girl!

She hit the accelerator. The snarl fell back, and she heard the scrabbling of claws just behind her. In one motion Dee opened her own door and vaulted out.

To-jin-ho was the art of falling on hard surfaces. Dee took this fall rolling and was on her feet in time to see the Spider cruise into the block wall of the garage.

Some distant part of her mind watched the impact with a sort of joyful awe. Now *there* was a crash, she thought, and flashed a barbaric smile at nothing.

Then she saw movement. Something was emerging from the Spider. She heard a rising snarl.

Dee spun on her heel and ran.

She could see the light of the stairwell in front of her. If she could make it there—

She felt her Nikes rebound from the concrete, felt her arms swinging, her lungs pumping. Her teeth drew back again in a grin. In that moment Dee

Eliade was filled with a joy in living so intense she felt she could fly.

"C'mon, you freakin' fleabag!" she shouted over her shoulder and heard herself laugh wildly. "Come and get me!"

She'd never fought a four-legged opponent before, but she was sure going to give it a try. She'd see how a wolf reacted to a roundhouse kick.

She reached the stairwell and spun, still laughing. The blood was singing in her veins, every breath she took was sweet. Her muscles were electric with vibrant energy. She felt balanced and dynamic and ready for anything.

Then she heard the creak of a door behind her— and an endless, savage hiss.

Michael was picking himself up as Jenny and Tom turned the corner, staring into the depths of the dim garage. He was clutching at one ankle.

"Dee—?" Jenny gasped. Echoes of a metallic crash were still reverberating in her mind.

Michael waved toward the back of the garage. Jenny saw it then—a large, dim shape against the wall. The Spider.

The lights flickered and went on, and she saw color.

The Spider's front end was crumpled. There was no sign of Dee.

"Come on!" Tom was already running toward the car. Then he looked left and shouted, "The stairway!"

The door there was swinging shut. Jenny heard it clang, felt her chest heave as they ran. Tom reached it and seized the handle with both hands, wrenching at it.

The door swung open, slamming against the wall. A single fluorescent panel flickered high above in the stairwell, and Jenny could hear echoes of her own panting breath in the little room. But nothing moved except shadows.

Dee's paper doll was on the floor, in a lightly scorched circle on the concrete.

"He's going to get us all."

Jenny tightened the Ace bandage around Michael's ankle.

"If Dee couldn't get away from them, what kind of chance do we have?"

Jenny fixed the little metal clips in the bandage and sat back.

"The clues aren't *fair*," Michael said. He was still breathing hard, and his eyes were too wide, showing white around the dark irises. "You said you and Tom ran straight down there once you got this one—which means you didn't have *time*. He's not going to give any of us enough time. And we're never going to find the base."

Jenny closed the plastic first aid kit. The paper doll was lying on the coffee table beside it. On its back, which wasn't characteristic of Dee at all. The black crayon eyes stared up at the ceiling with a crafty look.

They had pushed Audrey's car to the very back of the garage, where they hoped no one would find it. Jenny supposed they were lucky no one had come to investigate the crash—but did it really matter anymore? Did anything really matter?

"Am I just talking to myself here? Isn't anybody going to say something?"

Jenny looked at Michael, then at Tom, who was pacing the hall, not looking at them. She turned back to Michael, and her eyes met his. Their gazes locked a moment, then he sank back on the couch, his anger fading.

"What is there to say?" Jenny said.

They spent the evening in silence; Tom pacing and Michael and Jenny sitting. Staring at a blank TV screen.

It was all going to come crashing down soon—their carefully built structure of deception. Jenny had called her aunt Lily to say that Zach was upset and was spending the night with Tom. She'd called Dee's mother and told her Dee was staying with her. Neither mother had been happy. It was only a matter of time before one of them called Tom's house or Jenny's house and everything came out.

And Michael was right. They weren't going to find the base—not on the information they had now. They needed more.

She was actually glad that night when Julian showed up in her dreams.

It had taken her a long time to get to sleep—she'd lain for hours staring at the empty couch where Dee should have been. The last clear thing she remembered was deciding she was never going to sleep at all that night—and then she must have shut her eyes. When she opened them, she knew she hadn't really opened them at all. She was dreaming again.

She was standing in a white room. Julian was standing in front of a table, with the oddest thing stretched out in front of him. It was a sort of model, with houses and trees and roads and street lights. Like a railway model, only without the train, Jenny thought. But it was the most elaborate model she'd ever seen; the miniature trees and bushes were exquisitely made, and the little houses had various windows alight.

Not just a model, Jenny realized. It's Vista Grande —it's my neighborhood. There's my house.

Julian was holding a small figure of a wolf above one of the streets. He set it down carefully, looked up at Jenny, and smiled.

Jenny didn't smile back. Although she was dreaming, her head was clear—and she had a purpose in mind. She was going to get all the information she could from him.

"Is that how you tell them what to do? The wolf and the snake?"

"Possibly." He added, just as seriously as she had asked her question, "What's black inside, white outside, and hot?"

Jenny, mouth opened to speak again, shut it and gave him the kind of look Audrey frequently gave Michael. "What?" she said tightly.

"A wolf in sheep's clothing."

"Is that what you are?"

"Me? No, I'm a wolf in wolf's clothing." He looked up at her, and light flashed in his wild, exotic sapphire eyes.

I don't know how I ever mistook him for a human, Jenny thought. Julian was from an older and wilder race. One that had fascinated and terrified humans from the beginning.

I will not be distracted, she told herself. Not this time. I will remember what I want from him.

"What do you think of the new Game?"

"It isn't fair," Jenny said promptly. "Isn't *sporting,*" she added, remembering what Julian thought of the idea of fairness. "It's not a game at all if we don't have a chance to find your base."

"And you think you don't have a chance?"

"Not without some kind of information."

Julian threw back his head and laughed, his hair shining like white jade. "You want a hint?" He looked at her with those veiled, liquid-blue eyes.

"Yes," Jenny said flatly. "And you'd give it to me if you wanted it to be any kind of real contest. But you probably don't."

He clicked his tongue at her. "You really think I'm an ogre, don't you? But I'm not so bad. You know, if I wanted, I could manipulate the Game so I couldn't lose. For instance . . ." He lifted the wolf and held it judiciously over another street. Jenny recognized the pale gray wood-frame house and the tiny towheaded figure in front of it.

"Cam!" She looked at Julian. "You wouldn't! You said—"

His long lashes drooped. "I said I'd keep this Game to the original players—and I will. I'm just telling you what I *could* do. So you see I'm not so bad after all."

"Gordie Wilson wasn't a player."

"He put his nose in where he wasn't wanted."

"And what about P.C. and Slug?"

Julian's smile was chilling. "Oh, they were players, all right. They played their own game—and they lost."

So now I know, Jenny thought. I suppose I'll have to tell Angela—if I live to do it.

She was staring down at the tiny towheaded figure of Cam when something else occurred to her. She looked up.

"Was it you who made those kids play lambs and monsters?" she asked. "All that violence—were you influencing them?"

"Me?" He gave his black velvet laugh again. "Oh, Jenny—they don't need me. Children are that way naturally. Children's games are that way. Haven't you noticed?"

Jenny had, but she said nothing. She turned away.

"War and hunting and chasing—that's all there is. That's life, Jenny—no one can escape it."

He was standing behind her now.

"And why should we? There's excitement in the chase, Jenny. It gets the blood going. It sends chills through the body. . . ."

Jenny stepped away. *Her* blood was going. His voice, strange and haunting as the melody she'd heard on the hotel balcony at the prom, sent a shiver of awareness through her.

Cat-quiet, he followed her. I will not turn around, she thought. I will not.

"Love and death are everything, Jenny. Danger is the best part of the game. I thought you knew that."

Part of her did. The wild part that he had changed. The part of her, Jenny thought suddenly, that would always belong to him.

"And *I* thought you were going to give me a hint," she said.

"Of course, if you want—but nothing is free."

Jenny nodded without turning. She'd expected this. "Give the hint first," she said flatly.

"You can find your friends behind a door."

Jenny frowned. "What kind of a door? Have I seen it?"

"Yes."

"Have I been through it?"

"Yes—and no."

"What kind of an answer is that?" she said, angry enough to turn. She could face him when she was furious.

"It's as clear as black and white—if you know the right way to look at it. Now," he said, "the price." He stepped to her and bent his head.

It took all her self-control to remain rigid and unresponsive in his arms. At last she gasped and pulled away.

"Oh, Jenny. Let's stop playing—we don't need to play this Game anymore. You can have your friends back—you want Dee back, don't you?"

"I'll get her back," Jenny said shakily. She still felt tingles of electricity in every place Julian had touched her. "I'll get them all back—my way."

"As usual, I admire your confidence," he said. "But you can't win. Not against me, Jenny. I'm the master player."

"A door I've been through but haven't been through," she said. "A door that needs to be looked at in the right way."

He smiled. "A door in the shadows. But you won't find it until I take you through it."

We'll see, Jenny thought. Things were getting blurry around her—the shadows were growing. The dream fading.

"Here," Julian said. "To remember me by."

He put a silver rose in her hand.

176

Jenny recognized it. It was the rose he had given her in the Erlking's cavern, a shimmering half-open blossom, perfect down to the tiniest detail. The petals cool but soft in her palm.

There was something like a slip of white paper wrapped around the stem.

This time I'm going to wake up right away, she thought.

She did. The silver rose was lying on her pillow. She almost knocked it off, sitting up quickly to look at the bundles of blankets on the living room floor.

Tom and Michael were both there. Two dark heads on white pillows. Jenny leaned over and shook the nearest shoulder.

"Michael, Tom, wake up. I've got the next clue."

But when she unraveled the slip of paper from the stem, she wasn't sure.

"It's French," Michael said. "And none of us speaks French. It isn't fair."

"Life isn't fair," Jenny muttered, staring at the words on the paper in frustration. There were only six of them.

Pas de lieu Rhône que nous.

"If we only had Audrey," she said. *"Nous* means 'we,' I think—or is it 'you'?"

"Maybe Dad's got a French-English dictionary somewhere," Michael said.

Tom didn't even try to join in the conversation. He had looked at the silver rose, and then at Jenny, and then he had settled back. Now he was staring down at his own hands.

Jenny started to speak to him, then stopped. As she'd told Michael before, what was there to say?

The ring felt as cold as ice and as heavy as lead on her finger.

Michael found the French dictionary the next morning, but Jenny still couldn't make much sense of the clue. The words were French, but they didn't seem to make any sense when you put them together.

"It's about me, I know it is," Michael said. "Because it's French, and Audrey's connected with French, and I'm connected with Audrey. I'm next."

"You're ridiculous," Jenny said. "We don't know which of us it is—but if we all stay together—"

"Staying together didn't do Michael and Dee much good," Tom said from what had become his habitual position, pacing the hallway.

"He's going to get us all. One by one," Michael said softly. "And I'm next."

Jenny stared down at the dictionary and rubbed her eyes.

It was dark and stuffy in the apartment. Outside the sky was cloudy, gray as concrete. Jenny felt like a rat in a trap.

She tried thinking about the base instead of the French clue. She'd told Michael and Tom what Julian had said about the door, but none of them could make anything of it. Now Tom was pacing endlessly, and Michael was staring at nothing, and Jenny was very tired.

Her head felt stuffy and her eyes hurt. She'd had almost no sleep last night. Maybe if she shut her eyes she could think better. If she shut them just for a few minutes . . .

The crash woke her up with a jerk.

"Sorry," Michael whispered guiltily, picking up a

TV tray. He looked even more nervous than usual—almost wild. His hair was sticking up all over his head, and his eyes reminded Jenny of a hamster she'd once had—a frantic hamster that had always tried to run away from her.

"What time is it?" Jenny whispered back, trying to clear her head. It was almost as dark as night.

"About four. You slept for a while."

Jenny wondered vaguely why they were whispering, then saw the bundle of blankets on the floor in Tom's place. He was wrapped like a mummy, even his head covered.

Good—he needs rest, too, Jenny thought, shifting. The slip of paper rustled on her lap. Jenny's blurred eyes focused on the writing on it, her foggy brain seeing the words not as words but merely as letters—sounds. *Pas de lieu* . . .

She straightened suddenly, her breath hissing. Michael nearly jumped out of his skin.

"What is it?" He limped hastily over to her. "What—did you figure it out? Is it me?"

"Yes—oh, we've been so stupid, Michael. We didn't need the dictionary. It's not French at all."

"Even I can recognize that much French."

Jenny clutched at his arm. "The *words* are French, but it isn't a French sentence. I figured that out with the dictionary—the words don't make any sense when you put them together. It only makes sense in *English.*"

"What are you talking about, English?" Michael forgot to whisper.

"Just say the words to yourself, Michael. Pronounce them the French way, but kind of run them together."

"*Pas . . . de . . . lieu . . . Rhône . . . que . . . nous*—it doesn't say anything!"

"Yes, it does. It says 'Paddle your own canoe.'"

Michael's lips formed the words silently as he stared at the paper, then he hit himself in the forehead. "Oh, my God. You're right. But, Jenny"—he dropped his hand and looked at her—"what does it *mean?*"

"I don't know." Jenny glanced out the window, where large drops were hanging from the eaves of the walkway and small drops pattered on the concrete. "But it's got something to do with water, I bet—so none of us can go outside. But don't you realize, Michael"—she turned to him excitedly—"we've done it! We've finally done it! We have a clue, and we have all of *us* here and safe. We can win this one!"

Something about Michael's expression made her heart jolt.

And then she realized—she and Michael hadn't been whispering for some time. They'd almost been shouting—but Tom's blankets hadn't stirred.

"Michael—" He was staring at her in terror. The hamster look again. In a single motion Jenny darted to seize Tom's blankets, to yank them away.

She just stared at the bunched-up pillows underneath. She could feel herself folding inside. Collapsing.

"Michael." She spoke without moving, still holding the blankets. Then she lifted her head and looked at him. He flinched and raised a hand defensively.

"Where is he, Michael?"—deceptively softly.

"He made me, Jenny—I told him not to, but he wouldn't listen—"

"*Michael, where is he?*" Somehow Jenny had gotten two fistfuls of Michael's gray sweatshirt, and she was shaking him. "Where did he go?"

Speechlessly Michael looked toward the gray and dripping window. There were tears in his dark spaniel eyes.

"He went to the mountains," he gasped after a moment. "You know the place he told us about—where they found Gordie Wilson. He thought he could find the base there—or maybe just kill the wolf or the snake. He said that killing them might help you and me, even if he—" He stopped and began again. "I told him not to, Jenny—I told him not to go—"

Jenny heard her own voice, sounding strangely quiet and detached. Almost musical. "To the mountains. Where they found Gordie Wilson—in a creek bed. Isn't that right, Michael?"

Michael blinked at the lines of slanting gray outside. "In a creek . . ." he whispered.

Then they just looked at each other.

"Come on," Jenny said at last. "We've got to find him."

"He told me to keep you here—"

"Nothing will keep me here. I'm going, Michael. The only question is whether you're going with me."

Michael gulped, then said, "I'm going."

"Then let's get out of here. We may already be too late."

14

Tom had never shot a gun before. He'd taken this rifle from a case in Zach's father's den. Zach's father wasn't going to be happy when he found it missing, or when he found the back door jimmied open, either.

But Tom wasn't going to be around to hear about it.

He had no illusions on that. If he was right, this was strictly a one-way trip.

Of course, Julian's base might not be up here after all. There weren't any doors on this mountain slope, and Julian had told Jenny the others were behind a door. But this was definitely a place where the wolf and the snake hung out—and Tom didn't expect them to pass up the chance to attack him.

If he even got one of them, Jenny's chances would be better. If he got both, maybe she could actually make it.

The idea had first come to him the night Audrey

had disappeared, when they'd all been talking in Michael's living room. Michael and Dee had been saying that the only way to win Julian's game was to find the base, and Tom had said, *"There might be another way"*—and then stopped. The other way that he'd thought of was too dangerous. Too dangerous for Jenny, anyway. It wasn't a trip he wanted her making.

He'd thought about his idea during the next two days, going over it, debating about whether to tell Dee. She'd want to be in on it, he knew. But that would mean leaving Jenny practically unprotected. That was the basic problem with the idea—if Tom left Jenny, he left her vulnerable.

Then Dee had disappeared—and suddenly the choice had become critical. Soon Jenny wouldn't have *anyone* to protect her . . . and Julian could creep in through her dreams.

That was what had decided Tom in the end. He couldn't keep Julian out of the apartment—which meant he was no good to Jenny there. What he could do—maybe—was to give her one less enemy to fight.

I'll bet it took both of them—the wolf and the snake—to get Dee, he thought, trudging through the damp and puddling creek bed. Dee could've stood up to either one of them alone—but not both.

Maybe Jenny would have a chance against one or the other of them alone. Or maybe—if Tom's luck *really* held—he could get both before Julian killed him.

No one else had even suggested going after the animals. It simply hadn't occurred to them. They all thought of the creatures as phantoms—and, God, no wonder. The Shadow Wolf Tom had seen on the beach had looked like a moving nightmare, a luminous specter. But it had been flesh and blood.

That was what Tom's first trip out here had shown. The black and tarry stuff he'd scraped off that rock was blood. Gordie must have wounded one of the animals before it got him. The creatures could bleed —as Tom had proved for himself on the beach. He'd cut the wolf, and his knife had come away dark.

They could bleed, and they left physical marks behind, like the scratches on Audrey's car. They had some sort of material existence. Maybe they could die.

Tom was going to find out.

Rain was splattering his face. Cold rain, stinging drops—not like a spring shower. The cattails in the creek bed were swaying and dripping. Everything was gray.

He was getting near the place. Not far now. Tom was coming from the south, downwind of the three sycamores. Maybe he could surprise them.

In the gray cold he comforted himself with a picture of Jenny. Jenny—all warmth and sunlight. Golden-glowing, her hair streaming back in the wind. Jenny in the summertime, safe and happy and laughing. That was what Tom wanted—for Jenny to see another summer. In this world instead of the world of ice and shadows.

Even if he wasn't there to see it with her.

Movement ahead. Tom squinted into the rain, then smiled grimly. Yes, it was there. Black against the gray background, impossibly big, glowing with its own blue light like a rotten log full of foxfire. A creature that looked like a wolf painted with luminous paint on darkness. The sight of it alone was enough to send a human running and screaming, mind broken.

Because it wasn't real—it was *super*-real. It was the archetypical Wolf—the one kids dreamed about. The one that had inspired stories like Little Red Riding-Hood. The one that lurked at the back of the human brain, eternally crouched and ready. Reminding people of what the world had once been like, a savage place where humans were the prey. When teeth and claws came at you in the night, and you got *eaten*.

Funny, Tom thought, how most people these days took it for granted that they weren't going to get eaten. Not so long ago—a few thousand years, maybe—it had been a pretty serious problem. A constant danger, the way it still was for birds and kittens and mice and gazelles.

The sight of the Lurker, the Shadow Wolf, brought it all back clearly. One look at it and your brain stem remembered everything. How it felt to be chased by something that wanted to tear into your entrails. By something you couldn't bargain with, couldn't reason with, something without mercy to appeal to. Something only interested in tearing your flesh off in chunks.

Tom couldn't let a thing like that near Jenny.

He was almost close enough now. It was moving toward him, slowly, crouched. He could hear the thick snarls over the patter of rain.

Tom raised the gun to his shoulder.

Careful—steady. He was pretty good at this at carnivals, an excellent shot. The wolf was almost in range. Tom centered the crosshairs—

—and heard a noise behind him.

A slithering, dragging noise. The Creeper. The Snake.

He didn't turn. He knew that it was almost on him, that if he didn't run now—this instant—it would get him. He didn't turn. With every ounce of his will, he kept his eyes on the wolf.

In range. *Now! Now!*

A horrifying hiss right behind him—

Ignoring it, Tom squeezed the trigger.

The recoil staggered him. Carnival guns didn't buck like that. But the wolf was more than staggered. The force of the bullet dropped it in its tracks.

Got it! I got it! I did it—

The snake struck.

Tom felt the blow in the middle of his back. Already off balance, he fell. But he twisted even as he went down. One more shot—if he could get off one more shot—

He was lying in the mud. The snake was towering over him, a column of swaying darkness. Huge, and hugely powerful. Eyes shining with an unearthly light, mouth wide in a hiss. Giant dark head rearing back to strike—

Now! For Jenny—

Tom fired straight into the gaping mouth.

The snake's head exploded.

It was terrible. Dark blood spurted everywhere, stinging Tom's face, blinding him. Heavy coils, whipping in their death throes, fell on top of him, flogging him. He couldn't get them off. Everything was blood and darkness and struggling terror.

But I did it, Tom thought, clawing wildly at the flailing, spurting length of the snake. Oh, God, if I can just get out of here . . . *I did it*. They're dead.

That was when he heard the noise.

A roaring like a waterfall in the distance—or a river. Getting closer fast. And he couldn't see, couldn't get up.

Jenny, Tom thought—and then the water reached him.

"Jenny, you're scaring me," Michael said. It was almost a whimper.

Jenny herself wasn't scared. She was cold and clear and furiously angry.

The idea that Julian's base might be at the creek had passed through her mind once or twice. But she'd dismissed it last night because it didn't fit in with the door.

Tom had obviously felt differently.

"Keep walking," she said. It seemed as if they'd been walking forever. She knew they were in the right area because they'd found Tom's car—but where was the creek bed? Michael was limping badly.

"What's that?"

It was a rushing, liquid sound, louder than the rain. Jenny knew what she would see even before they crested the next rise of ground and looked down.

An unusual sight for southern California, where most creek beds were cracked and dusty. This one was full of dark, swiftly moving water—much too full for the little rain that had fallen. There was no natural explanation for it. It was a freak event, a flash flood that should have been impossible.

But it was there. A swollen river by a sage-covered slope leading to three large sycamore trees.

And in a little eddy directly below Jenny, swirling

187

round and round between some rocks, was a neatly folded paper boat manned by a dark-haired paper doll.

She didn't realize the boat was the next clue until they were back at the apartment.

She had been playing with it all the way. She'd set Tom's doll on the coffee table with the others, arranging them with mad precision beside the car keys Michael had thrown there. A little line of paper dolls that sat and looked at her as she sat on the couch. She'd been turning the boat over and over in her hands while Michael huddled in a blanket on the love seat.

Then she saw the writing on the waxy paper.

It was very simple, a kid's riddle. The simplest clue of all.

What gets bigger the more you take away from it?

She'd heard that one in kindergarten, and both she and Michael knew the answer.

A hole.

"It doesn't say who's next—but I guess it doesn't need to," Michael said, pulling the blanket closer around him. "He'll save you for last—the best for last, you know. So it's me. And it doesn't say how it's going to happen, but that doesn't really matter, does it? As long as you know it's going to happen, and it is. We know that, huh, Jenny? It's going to happen, and there's nothing we can do to stop it. That Julian, he's like the Mounties, he always gets his man. . . ." He began to giggle.

"Michael, calm down. . . ."

"So there's a hole somewhere, and I'm going to fall into it. That's all we need to know. That's all, folks."

"Maybe not. You said Tom went to get the snake or the wolf—maybe he did. And the base wasn't there, but maybe we can still find it."

"May be, may be—it's still May, isn't it?" He looked at the curtained window. It was fully dark outside. He turned back to Jenny. "You know we're never going to find it."

"I *don't* know that." Jenny's hands were icy cold, but her voice was fierce. "I have an idea—something else Julian said. Something about the hint being as clear as black and white. And before, in my first dream, he said something about image and reality."

"What is this reality thing, anyway?" Michael said. "I mean, how do we know we ever got out of the paper house? Maybe this is all an illusion, like when you think you've woken up but you're still dreaming. Maybe we're still in the old Game. Maybe nothing is solid." He leaned over and hit the coffee table and giggled again.

"Michael, why don't you lie down? Look, I'll get you some water—"

"No! Don't leave me!" He clutched at her as she went by. "If you leave me, he'll get me! The Shadow Man will get me!"

"Okay, Michael. Okay." Jenny looked down into the terrified dark eyes and stroked Michael's hair as if he were younger than Joey. "Okay."

"It's not okay. I have to go to the bathroom—but he can get me there, too."

"No, look, I'll go with you. I'll stand right outside the door."

"He'll get me. Didn't you ever hear about snakes coming out of the toilet? He'll get me, but I have to go. . . . What a dilemma, huh? Let him get me or bust." Michael was almost crying, even while he continued to giggle.

"Michael, stop it. Stop it!" For the second time that day Jenny shook him. "Just calm down! The potty monster is not going to get you, I promise. We'll look for snakes before you go. Let's do it now and get it over with, and then we can think about the base."

Michael shut his eyes and gulped in a deep breath. When he let it out, he seemed calmer. "Okay." But he still staggered like somebody half-asleep when Jenny led him to the bathroom.

"You see? No snakes in there. And I'll stand right outside."

"Leave the door open a crack."

"Okay, Michael." Jenny stood patiently.

"Jenny?" Michael's voice behind the door sounded very small. "A toilet's a lot like a hole. . . ."

"Just do it, Michael!"

"Okay." After a minute the toilet flushed.

"You see? You're all right."

Michael didn't answer. The toilet went on flushing.

"Michael?"

The sound of rushing water.

"Michael, it's not funny! Come out of there, or I'm coming in."

The water rushed on.

"*Damn* it, Michael! All right, I warned you—" She jerked the door open.

The bathroom was empty. The toilet was flushing madly, water swirling round and round. Perched on the edge of the porcelain seat was a paper doll.

* * *

Five little dollies all in a row. Audrey sitting with her arm twisted up as if to say, "Can we talk?" Zach with his pencil-shaded face looking sharp and malicious. Dee, who kept falling on her back no matter how Jenny folded her. Tom, with a drop or two of rain still beaded on his wax. And Michael, whose crayon eyes seemed to stare at Jenny in accusation.

She'd promised it wouldn't get him, and it had.

Jenny was guilty, just as she was guilty of Summer's death. Not in the sense the police had meant, not the hacking-off-Summer's-head-and-burying-her-body-in-the-backyard sense, but because she was the one who'd gotten Summer into it. Jenny had invited Summer to play a game that had turned out to be deadly. Jenny had come out alive and Summer hadn't. Jenny's Game had killed Summer.

Now it might have killed the rest of her friends.

And she was alone. The apartment practically echoed with aloneness. There was no sound since she had jammed a book under the toilet ball to keep it from flushing anymore.

The rest of them had been picked off one by one. Like ten little Indians. Now she was the only one left, and she was next.

The base. I have to find the base. I have to get them out before Julian gets me.

But how?

The hints. She had to remember them. But her mind was so confused. She was all alone—she could feel the air around her. She could *feel* how each room in the apartment was empty. The emptiness was crushing her.

The hints. Think of them, nothing else. Get them in mind.

191

But I'm alone—

Image as opposed to reality.

A door she'd seen. A door she'd been through, but hadn't been through.

Not in the Shadow World. Maybe somewhere halfway.

What else was halfway? Like the More Games store—

Black and white.

A tiny light went on in Jenny's mind. Yes. It would fit. A door she'd seen and gone through—but that she couldn't possibly have gone through, depending on how you looked at it. A black and white door.

It was just then that the piece of paper came fluttering down.

From nowhere. It came out of thin air as if someone had dropped it from the ceiling. It skimmed and side-slipped and landed almost in her lap.

Jenny picked it up and looked at the writing.

I'm something. I'm nothing.
I am short. I am tall.
When you fall at your sport, then I stumble and fall.
I have never been seen yet beneath a new moon.
I thrive in the evening but vanish at noon.
I am lighter than air, I weigh less than a breath;
Darkness destroys me, and light is my death.

A little over three weeks ago Jenny might have had trouble with that one. What could be destroyed by both light and darkness? What could be both short and tall? What was something and nothing at once?

But ever since April 22, the day of the Game, the subject of this particular riddle had been on Jenny's mind. She'd been haunted by it, she'd thought about almost nothing else.

She saw shadows everywhere these days.

She had no doubt about what the riddle meant, either. A shadow was coming to get her—*the* shadow. The Shadow Man. Julian was going to take care of this personally.

She had barely thought this when all the lights in the apartment went out.

Chills swept over Jenny. Icy fingers stirred the hairs at the back of her neck. Her palms were tingling wildly.

I'm in trouble. Bad trouble. But I think I know the answer now. I know where the base is. If I can just get there . . . if I can get to it before he gets to me. . . .

First, find the way out of the apartment.

There was some light coming in through the curtains from the walkway. All right—the front door was over there. Jenny picked up Michael's keys and made her way to it, arms outstretched.

As she reached the walkway, the lights there went out.

Cat and mouse. He's playing games with me. All right, play! This mouse is running.

Her hand slid on the wet iron railing as she hurried down the stairs. In the carport Michael's VW Bug was swathed in shadows. Jenny pulled the door open and slipped in, turning the key in the ignition almost before the door was shut. She pulled out just as the parking lot lights went off.

Right behind me . . .

She wrenched the wheel and sped out of the apartment complex.

The rain had started again, droplets splattering the windshield. Hard to drive safely. Jenny sped on, hoping no one was in her way.

A stoplight—the brakes screeched. Please, God, don't let me hit anyone. Please—

The red light winked out, but the green didn't come on. The stoplight stayed dark, swaying in the rain.

Jenny hit the accelerator.

Canyonwood Avenue—Sequoia Street—Tassajara . . .

The Bug's engine coughed.

No—let me make it. I've got to make it. I'm so close—

Jacqueline Drive . . .

The engine coughed again.

Quail Run! Jenny took the turn dangerously fast, tires skidding. The Bug lurched and a horrible grinding sound came from the engine. Still skidding, it hit the curb—and stopped.

Frantically Jenny turned the key. She got a squeal of metal that set her teeth on edge. Then silence.

Get out! Quick!

Abandoning the key, she fumbled with the door, jumped into the rain. She left the door open and ran.

Up there, just a few more houses. Go, go! She made her legs pump, flying over the wet sidewalk. Don't look back! Don't think! Just go!

There it is! You can see it! A few more yards—

Lungs burning, she reached the driveway of the mock Tudor house. Zach's house. The driveway was empty. She staggered to the garage, seized the handle in the middle of the big door. She pulled as hard as she could.

It was stuck fast. Locked.

Oh, God! Don't panic. The side door, quick!

As she started for it, she could see down Quail Run, could see the deserted Bug nosed against the curb under a streetlight.

The streetlight went out.

Then the next closest one did. Then the next.

A wave of darkness coming toward her. Bearing down on her. The side door was that way.

Jenny turned and ran toward the front door of the house.

She grabbed at the doorknob while knocking, and to her surprise it turned. It was unlocked. Were they crazy?

"Uncle Bill! Aunt Lily! It's me!"

She yelled because she didn't want them to shoot her for a burglar, and because she didn't care about keeping her secret any longer. She desperately wanted people, any people.

The house echoed emptily in answer.

"Uncle Bill! Aunt Lily!"

The silence was ponderous, a tangible presence. There was no one here. For some unfathomable reason they had gone away, leaving their front door unlocked. Jenny was alone.

I won't cry. I won't scream. I just have to get to the garage, that's all. Nothing's changed. I can get there easily. It's just the length of the house away.

Her heart was frozen in panic.

Just go! One foot in front of the other. It's just an empty house!

The hallway light went off.

Oh, my God—he's here! Oh, God, he's *here*, he's in the house, he's got me—

Go!

She stumbled into the darkness, heading for the lighted living room. Her legs were shaking so badly she could hardly walk. Her outstretched hands were numb.

She got one glimpse of the living room, then the brass lamp beside the leather couch went out. She banged into a wastebasket made of an elephant's foot—a thing that had always filled her with horror. She could hardly keep from screaming.

Every inch of her skin was tingling. Shrinking—as if expecting an attack from any side.

It was pitch dark. He could be anywhere around her. Anywhere in the darkness, moving quietly as a shadow himself. If she took a step, she might run right up against him.

She had to do it. She had to find the garage. For Tom—for Dee. They were waiting for her to rescue them. She'd promised Michael . . .

Sobbing without making a noise, she took a step.

Now another one, she ordered herself. Feel your way. But it was almost more than she could do to reach out into that darkness. Anything might grab her hand. She might reach out and feel *anything*. . . .

Do it!

She took another step, groping blindly. Shuffling across the floor. Her hand struck a wall, with emptiness beside it.

The entrance to the dining room. That's it. And the garage is just on the other side, through the kitchen. You can make it.

She shuffled into the dining room, one hand on the cool smoothness of wallpaper. She could feel the immensity of the darkness on her exposed side. Something could come at her from that side—

—or from the wall. Oh, God, he makes things come out of walls. Jenny snatched her hand away from the wallpaper. Nothing was safe. He could grab her from any direction.

Just go!

She staggered forward in the dark and found another empty space—the doorway to the kitchen. Thank God. Now just a few more steps. Turn left around the refrigerator. Good. Now the way was clear until the garage—

She stepped against something warm and hard in the darkness. She screamed.

"You didn't think," the voice like water over rock said gently, "that I would actually let you get there, did you?"

He was holding her by the upper arms, not roughly but inescapably. Jenny's eyes were filled with darkness, and the rushing of her own blood filled her ears.

"Actually, I'm surprised you got this far. I didn't think you would—but I got your aunt and uncle out of the way just in case. An urgent message from their missing son."

I'm going to faint. I really am, this time.

Jenny couldn't keep her knees steady. He was half supporting her now.

"Shh. You don't need to cry. You've lost the Game, that's all. It's over now."

Dark. She was in complete darkness. She looked around wildly, turning as far as he would let her. If she could only see a tiny light—but there was nothing. The wolf and the snake weren't here; she would have seen their sickly, phosphorescent glow. She was alone with the Shadow Man.

And he was going to take her.

"Oh, God, where are we? Are we there already—at the base?" she said hysterically. It was impossible to tell in this complete darkness.

"No. Shh, shh, Jenny. We're going in a moment. You see, here's the way."

Then Jenny did see a light—just a glimmer. A weird, eldritch light like blue electricity. Defining a space opening in the floor behind Julian. A gap, a vortex. A hole.

15

No . . . Jenny couldn't stand to look at the hole. She turned from it and buried her face in Julian's chest.

"It's all right. Just a little step. Then we'll be together, Jenny." He tipped her face up in the darkness, touching it with fingertips cool as marble.

His touch—so light, so certain. Commanding. As if he could see easily in this utter blackness. So cool. His fingertips traced her wet cheekbone, thumb wiping away the tears. Jenny shut her eyes involuntarily.

"Together, forever."

The cool fingertips brushed over her eyelashes, stroked the hair back from her temple. She felt one trace her eyebrow.

"It was meant to be, Jenny. You know that. You can't fight it any longer."

The finger ran down her cheek like a cool tear. It traced the outline of her lips, the join between upper and lower. A touch so light she could barely feel it. It took the bones out of her legs.

Melting, falling . . .

"Come with me, now, Jenny." His fingertips brushed the line of her jaw, sending delightful shivers through her. She realized her head had fallen back. Her face was turned up as if for a kiss. "I'll go with you. It's time to concede the Game. To surrender . . ."

A tiny light went on in Jenny's mind.

No wolf and no snake. And they were still in Zach's kitchen, which she knew very well. And the hole was behind Julian—and just beyond that the garage door . . .

"All right," she whispered. "All right, but let go of me. I can walk."

Dee always said surprise was the most important element of any attack. Don't give your opponent a second to consider.

The instant Julian's grip loosened, Jenny shoved him.

She didn't think about it, she just pushed as hard as she could. And he was taken by surprise. Even his snake-quick reflexes couldn't save him. With a shout the Shadow Man fell backward into his own black vortex.

Jenny leaped over the hole at the same moment.

A jump straight into darkness. If she'd miscalculated, she'd knock herself out against the wall. As it was her hands struck the door, almost upsetting her backward—but she kept her balance. Her fingers closed on the doorknob, she wrenched it—then she was in the garage.

Zach's flashlight would be on the wall. At least, she

prayed it still would be. She flew across the length of the garage recklessly, groping for it. Julian wouldn't take long to recover—he could be here any second—

Flashlight! Jenny thumbed the switch. She had never been so glad to see anything as she was to see the white circular beam that shot out. Light, at last, light.

She swung the beam to the wall, aiming with dead certainty at what she'd come for. The mural photograph Zach had taken of the high school cafeteria.

Julian had told her that black and white mixed make so many colors—but not in a photograph. A photograph—an image of reality—an image that included a door. The exit door that the pyramid of tables had almost blocked, a door in the shadows behind the tables. A door Jenny had been through in real life many times. But she'd never been through it—because you can't open a picture of a door.

Unless, like the mural on Montevideo Avenue, it was a door into unreality. Into a place halfway to the Shadow World, like the More Games store. Julian could make images into reality. He could make posters and murals come alive. If Jenny looked at this picture in the right way . . .

As Jenny stared at the door, the handle seemed to bulge out at her. Three-dimensional. Like the doorknob to the More Games store which had stuck out of the mural.

"Jenny!"

Julian's voice behind her, sharp and dangerous. The flashlight went out.

But Jenny had seen where the handle was. She reached for it in the darkness. Her fingers brushed it—it was cold. Real metal in her hand. She had it!

She pulled.

Rushing wind surrounded her. The cold metal seemed to melt from under her fingers, and she was falling. Her scream was snatched away by the thunder of the air.

She had never seen anyone look as surprised as Audrey and Zach and Dee and Tom and Michael did. Their five faces were turned toward her, staring, mouths and eyes open, as she staggered forward and landed on her knees.

Now, what just happened—? Jenny thought, but before she could look behind her, they were all around her.

"You came through the *door*," Audrey said, greatly excited. She was still wearing the black Oscar de la Renta dress Jenny had last seen her in, and it was more bedraggled than ever. Her copper hair was down.

"Are you all right?" Tom asked. There were muddy streaks on his cheekbones. He reached out to take her hand, her left hand, without seeming to care about the ring on it.

"Of course she's all right. She came through the door," Dee said gleefully. She patted Jenny's head in a frenzy of affection. "Eat that, monster!" she shouted to the ceiling.

"You lied to me," Michael said. He still had the hamster look, only now his lower lip was pushed out pathetically, too. "You said it wouldn't get me, and it did."

Jenny leaned against Tom's warmth and solidity and shut her eyes—which made tears trickle out.

She had never been so glad to hear Michael's complaining in her life.

"It's you—it's all of you," she said, opening her eyes with a little sob that sounded strange even to herself. "You're really here."

"Of course we're here," Audrey said. She sounded cross, which meant she was feeling affectionate. "Where else would we be?"

Dee grinned. "We've been waiting for you to come get us, Tiger. Didn't I say she would? Didn't I?"

Jenny looked at Zach. He had black circles under his eyes and his skin had a waxy tint, but there was something oddly peaceful in his expression. "Are you okay?" she said. "Are you all okay?"

Zach shrugged. "We're alive. It seems like a week we've been here, but Tom says it's only a couple of days. I just wish I could get back and develop these." He jangled the camera around his neck, and Jenny looked at him in surprise. "Got some great shots of that snake." His eyes met Jenny's, and he smiled.

Jenny smiled back.

"I was here alone first," Audrey was saying. "For more than a whole day. *That* was fun." She pressed her lips together.

"It's not so bad," Dee said. "It's sort of like the army. We sleep on the tables—see, there're blankets over there. And there's a bathroom, and food comes out *there*. A cafeteria's actually a pretty good place to keep people. But we never could get that door open, and none of us came in through it."

Jenny looked around. It was a cafeteria, all right. The Vista Grande High School cafeteria. Exactly like the photograph, except that the tables had been unstacked and the six of them were standing around. The only really peculiar thing was that there was only one door in all the four walls, the only door that had been visible in the picture.

"How did you guys get here, then?" she asked.

"Through the ceiling," Michael said grimly. "I kid you not."

Jenny blinked up at the ceiling. There was a large black hole in the center. Blue electricity crackled through the darkness.

Tom spoke quietly beside her. "We can't get up there. We tried. There aren't enough tables—and something really strange happens when you get anywhere near that high. Time seems to slow down and you start to pass out."

Jenny looked down from the hole. "But you're all okay. The snake and the wolf didn't hurt anybody?"

"No," Dee said. "They just wanted us to fall in the vortexes. And they're dead now, you know. Tom got 'em."

"I *think* I got them," Tom said cautiously. "Michael was just telling us that you hadn't seen them tonight. . . ."

"You did get them," Jenny said. "You must have, because they're gone. It was a stupid, *stupid* thing to do, going off alone like that"—she squeezed his hand hard—"but I'm glad you did, because if you hadn't I wouldn't be here. I had to jump over a hole—a vortex or whatever you call it—and if they'd been around, I'm sure they'd have chased me back in."

Dee looked interested. "So just where was Julian when you were jumping?"

"In the vortex. I pushed him."

Dee stared at her, then snorted with laughter. In a minute they were all laughing hysterically. Even Zach was chuckling. Dee punched Jenny in the arm.

"He's gonna be mad," Michael hiccuped weakly as the hysteria subsided.

"He is. What difference does it make?" Jenny said coolly. "I found the base. I won." She waved a hand at them. "All you little lambs are free." Then she looked around and waited.

Nothing happened.

Everyone settled back. The joyful frenzy showed the first cracks as they stared around them, waiting for some change. Tom's eyebrows were drawing together darkly. Dee's beautifully sculpted lips lifted to show teeth.

"Oh, you would, would you?" she said softly and dangerously to nothing. "You cheat."

"Maybe we have to yell," Michael said. "Oly-oly-oxen free!"

"Don't be stupid," said Zach. "We *are* in. We want to get out."

"And he's got to let us out," Jenny said. She stood up, looking at the hole in the ceiling. "It's the rules of the Game. Unless he *is* planning to cheat," she added loudly, feeling reckless and bold with Tom's hand in hers.

"I never cheat," Julian said, from behind them. "I practice Gamesmanship—the art of winning games without *actually* cheating."

Jenny turned. Julian was standing just in front of the door—which was now open. The red Exit sign blinked and glowed madly above it, looking as if it

205

would blow a fuse at any moment. That should have been a good omen, but the look on Julian's face wasn't encouraging at all. His eyes were glittering like blue glass, and there was something cruel and predatory about his mouth.

"Then you'll let us go," Jenny said, not quite so boldly as before. She steadied her voice and made herself meet his eyes, lifting her chin proudly. "I got in myself, Julian," she said. "I found the base."

"Yes, you did." Even here, in the well-lit cafeteria, it seemed like twilight around him. A strange, enchanted twilight that was somehow brighter and more real than any daytime Jenny had ever seen. "You found the base. You won the Game. Now all you have to do is walk out."

"While you block the door," Dee said scornfully. "Looks like you'll have to do it yourself this time, since your animal friends aren't here to do it for you."

"Block the door?" Julian widened his cat-tilted eyes innocently, somehow looking more disturbingly beautiful than ever. And more triumphant. "I wouldn't *dream* of it." He stepped away from the exit, gesturing with languid, careless grace, as if to usher them in. "Go on. All you have to do is walk through there, and you'll be outside the photograph. In Zach's garage. Safe and sound."

"I wouldn't trust him as far as I could throw him," Michael whispered in Jenny's ear. But Dee, always eager for a challenge, was already moving toward the door. She flashed an ebony glance toward Julian as she passed him, and he bowed gracefully. Then he lifted his head and smiled at Jenny, who was standing in the protective circle of Tom's arm.

"I told you once not to mess with me," he said. Under his heavy lashes his eyes were blue as flame.

Alarm spurted through Jenny. *"Dee—"* she began. But it was already happening.

Just as Dee reached the door, there was a tremendous sound—a sound that was both loud and soft at the same time. It was almost like the sound a gas burner makes when you turn it on and the gas ignites. A muffled *whompf.*

Only this was a hundred times louder, and it came from all around them. Jenny's ears popped. Heat struck her from every direction at once, and a blast of burning air sent her hair streaming straight upward.

Dee was thrown backward by the force of the explosion, breaking her fall by striking the ground first with her forearms and palms. The next instant Jenny was holding her, her voice hard with anxiety.

"Are you okay? Are you okay?"

Dee's sooty lashes fluttered. Her slim chest was heaving, and her neck, long and graceful as a black swan's, lay arched back on Jenny's arm.

"Dee!"

"I'll give him gamesmanship," Dee gasped at last. Her eyes opened into narrow onyx slits, her breath still hitching. "I'll give him gamesmanship right up the—"

"He's gone," Zach interrupted flatly. "And we're all in trouble, so I wouldn't waste your breath."

For a moment Jenny was so glad to see Dee unhurt that she didn't care. Then she looked up and understood what Zach meant.

They were inside a ring of fire.

It was just slightly smaller than the dimensions of

the cafeteria—and for all Jenny knew the cafeteria walls were still outside of it. You couldn't see through it to tell. It was as high as the cafeteria ceiling, and it was hot.

And *loud*.

Incredibly loud. Jenny realized that she and the others had been shouting over it to be heard. It made an unbelievable, unremitting roaring. Like the thundering of Niagara Falls, or the blast of a hurricane.

How weird, Jenny thought, part of her mind examining this fact with a curious calm. I guess when you get to a certain extreme, the elements all sound like one another—fire sounds like water sounds like wind. I'll have to remember that.

There was something else about the sound. It was deadly.

You knew, somehow, listening to it, that it was absolutely lethal. If destruction had a voice, this was it.

"I suppose that's why people jump out of windows, even from the twentieth floor, or whatever," she said to Tom, almost dreamily. "You know, from a burning building, I mean."

He gave her a sharp look, then lifted her, practically carrying her to one of the cafeteria tables. "Lie down."

"I'm all right—"

"Jenny, lie down before you pass out."

Jenny suddenly realized that she'd better. She was shaking violently all over, tiny tremors that seemed to come from deep inside her. Her fingers and lips were numb.

"She's in shock," Audrey said as Jenny lay back on

the bench. "And no wonder, after everything that's happened. Jenny, shut your eyes for a while. Try to relax."

Jenny shut her eyes obediently. She could see the fire just as well that way as with them open. A wave of dizziness rolled over her. She could hear the others speaking, but their shouts seemed thin and far away.

"—not going to last long with this heat," Tom was saying.

"No—but what can we *do?*" That was Zach.

"We're going to get *roasted.*" And that was Michael. "Better find some *mint* sauce."

"Shut up or I'll croak you myself, Mikey," Dee said.

I can't let them get roasted, Jenny thought. Her thoughts were vague and dreamlike, held together by the thinnest of floating strings. It was a state almost like the moments before sleep, when nonsense seems perfectly sensible, and words and pictures come from nowhere.

Right now she was experiencing something like drowning. Her life flashing before her—or at least the last three weeks—or at least bits of them. Disconnected, jumbled images, each sharp as a clip from a high-grade home video.

Julian appeared, beautiful as a December morning, his eyes like liquid cobalt, his hair moon-wet. *"I never cheat. I practice Gamesmanship. . . ."*

And Aba, her old face with its fine bones under velvety night-black skin. *"Last night I dreamed a Hausa story. . . ."*

And Michael, dear Michael, his hair wildly mussed, dark eyes shining with enthusiasm: *"See, your brain is like a modeling system. It takes the input from your senses and makes the most reasonable model it can. . . ."*

And Zach, thin and beaky-nosed, gray eyes alight with a fierce gleam. *"A picture of a pipe is not a pipe."*

As Jenny drifted, ears filled with the noise of the fire, all the images seemed to float together, merging and intertwining. As if Aba and Michael and Zach were speaking at once.

"Without another word the girl dived into the river of fire. . . ."

"Touching's just another sense. It could be fooled, too. . . ."

"The image isn't reality. Even though we're used to thinking that way. . . ."

"The fire burned her, of course—my mother always said 'The fire burned her like fire. . . .'"

"If a model's good enough, there would be no way to tell it wasn't real. . . ."

"We show a kid a picture of a dog and say 'This is a doggie'—but it's not. . . ."

Jenny sat up. The fire was burning as fiercely as ever, like all the beach bonfires in the world fused into one. Tom and Dee and the others were standing in a sort of football huddle a few feet away. Jenny felt light-headed but good. She felt light all over, in fact, as if carbonated bubbles were lifting her toward the ceiling, bursting inside her. She felt glorious.

"That's it," she whispered. "That's it."

She had to shout to make them hear her. "Tom. Tom, come here—everybody come here. I've got it. I know how to get out."

They crowded around her. "What?" "You're kidding!" *"Tell us."*

Jenny laughed for the sheer pleasure of laughing, feeling crystal clear and brilliant. Like a sphere filled with moonlight. She lifted her arms joyfully, shook back her hair, and laughed again.

The others exchanged glances, their expressions changing from excitement to consternation.

"No, it's okay," Jenny assured them. "I know how we get out—we just *walk.* Don't you see? The fire isn't real! It's a model our brains are making."

They didn't look nearly as happy as she would have thought. They blinked at her, then at one another. Michael opened his mouth and then shut it again, looking nervously at Audrey. Audrey sighed.

"Ah." Dee glanced at the others, then patted Jenny's shoulder. "Okay, Sunshine. You go back to sleep, and later we'll talk about it."

"What, you think I'm joking? I'm not. I'm telling you—we can walk right out of here."

"Uh, Tiger—" Dee looked over her shoulder at the fire, then back at Jenny. "I hate to tell you, but that fire is not a model in my brain. It's *hot.* I've got blisters." She showed Jenny several fluid-filled bumps on her hand.

Jenny looked at them, briefly shaken. Then she recovered. "That's because you let it happen. You believed in the heat, and it gave you blisters," she said. "No, Dee, don't humor me, damn it!" she added. "I'm serious. You know how hypnotized people can get a blister if you tell them that you're touching them with something hot—even if it isn't hot. It's like that."

Michael ran his hands through his hair. "No, but Jenny, it's *really* hot. You can't even get near it."

"That's because you *believe* it's hot. You were the

one who said it, Michael: If a model is good enough, you can't tell the difference between it and reality." She looked from one face to another. The glorious lightness had disappeared; now she felt crushing disappointment. "You think I'm crazy, don't you? All of you."

"Jenny, you've been through so much—"

"I don't want sympathy, Audrey! I want you to listen. Will *you* listen, Zach?" She turned to him desperately. "Remember Magritte? You told me that the image is not the reality, and I said, 'Unless you have somebody who can *make* an image into reality.' But what if that's not what Julian does? What if he doesn't make an image into reality, but he makes us *think* it's reality? If he shows our senses something so convincing that our brains make a model of it and believe it—even though it's just an illusion? Like a dream."

"'What if?'" Zach quoted back to her. "That's a pretty big *if*, Jenny. What if you're wrong?"

"Then we're toast," Michael muttered.

"But it's the only thing that makes *sense*," Jenny said. "Remember, Julian said he wouldn't actually cheat. If the fire's real and there's no way to get through it, then that's cheating. Right? Don't you think?"

"I think your faith in him is charming," Audrey said acidly, her copper-colored eyebrows raised. She looked at Tom, but Tom looked away. Refusing to side against Jenny—but not looking at Jenny, either.

"It's not just faith in him. It's *sense*," Jenny said. "Don't you see: Aba had a dream almost exactly like this. And the girl in that story came through all right. Her will was strong enough."

"But the fire burned her," Michael pointed out.

"But it didn't kill her. I'm not saying it won't hurt—I'm sure it will, from the look of Dee's blisters. But I don't think it will kill unless we let it. If our will is strong enough, we can get through." But she could see by their faces that they were still unconvinced.

Despair clutched at Jenny's chest. "Dee?" she said, almost pleading.

Dee shifted uncomfortably. "Sunshine—if it were anything else . . . but I've *been* there. It sure felt like a real fire to me. And even if I could convince myself to walk in—what happens if I get into the middle of it and my will suddenly isn't strong enough?"

". . . toast," Michael said.

Audrey spoke decisively. "It's too big a risk."

"When an illusion is that good," Zach said, "it might as well be real. It can still kill us."

Jenny stood.

"Okay," she said. "I understand—if it wasn't my own idea, I'd probably think it was crazy, too. And I'm the one who got you all into this, so it's only fair I get you out. I'm going in alone."

Tom's head jerked around. "Now, *wait* a minute—" he said at the same moment Zach said, "Now, look—"

"No, it's decided," Jenny said. "I have the best chance, since I'm the one who believes I can get through it."

"That's only if your theory is *right,*" Dee said, standing in front of Jenny to block her. "If you're wrong, you're *dead* wrong. No, Sunshine, you're not going anywhere."

"Yes, I am." Jenny leaned forward, eye to eye with

Dee, matching the other girl's volume and ferocity. "This is my decision. I'm going and no one is going to stop me. Get it?"

Dee let out her breath sharply. She glared—but she fell back to let Jenny pass. Michael, eyes wide, moved hastily out of the way, tugging Audrey with him. Even Zach, although his face was white and furious, recoiled a step, unable to hold Jenny's gaze.

It was Tom who caught Jenny's arm. "Just hang on a minute," he said, his voice reasonable. Jenny turned on him, holding her head up like a queen because she was frightened to death, because he was the only one here who might be able to undermine her determination. In her mind's eye she could see herself standing there, drawn up to her full height, with her hair loose on her shoulders in the firelight. She hoped she looked commanding. She felt tall and proud—and beautiful.

"I said nobody is going to stop me, Tom. Not even you."

"I'm not trying to stop you," Tom said, still quiet and reasonable. His hazel eyes were steady, almost luminous in the light of the fire, and his face was clear. Tranquil, with a look of utter conviction. "I'm going with you."

Jenny felt a rush of warmth and dizzy gratification. She grabbed his hand and squeezed hard. "You believe me!"

"Let's go." He squeezed her hand back, then looked at it and took the other one, the one with the ring. His fingers interlocked with hers, and Jenny felt strong enough to *jump* over the fire. "Come on."

They turned to face the fire together.

It was good that Jenny was feeling invulnerable

just then, because the fire was terrible. Hotter than putting your hand in an oven. Jenny could feel sweat trickle down her sides as they approached it; the skin on her face felt tight and hot and tingling.

"We'd better do it fast!" Tom shouted over the roar.

Jenny pointed with her free hand. "I think the door is *there.*"

"You guys, now, wait, you guys—" Michael was yelling.

Jenny looked at the firelight reflected in Tom's eyes. "One, two, *three—*" They nodded at each other and started for the flames, ignoring the panicked shouts behind them.

"Cool, wet grass! Cool, wet grass!" Tom shouted, and then the fire was all around them.

16

Jenny's skin burnt off.

That was what it felt like. As if it were flaying off in strips. Searing crisp and black until it cracked open. Charring. Frying like bacon. Her hair igniting, burning like a torch on her head.

It had been easy to say *"Just walk through the fire, it's a model, it isn't real."* But the moment she stepped into it, she understood what Dee meant about it *feeling* real. If she'd gotten close enough before to feel anything of this heat, she would never have dared to suggest it.

That first second was the most horrible thing that had ever happened to Jenny. It was agonizing—and she panicked. She lost her head completely. She'd been wrong, it wasn't an illusion after all, and she was in the middle of a *fire*. She was on fire. She had to run—to run—to get away from this. But she didn't know which way to go. The roaring, crackling, *killing* flames were all around her, burning her like a wax doll thrown in a furnace, roasting her alive.

I'm dying, she thought wildly. *I'm dying—*

Then she heard the faint shout from beside her: "Cool-wet-grass! Cool-wet-grass!"

And she felt Tom's hand in hers. Tom was pulling her, dragging her along.

I've got to make it—for Tom, she thought. If I collapse, he won't leave me. He'll die, too. We've got to keep going. . . .

Somehow she made her legs move, lunging desperately through the flames in the direction Tom was leading her. She just prayed it was the right direction.

"She was terribly afraid, but her love for the boy was stronger than her fear. . . ."

"Cool, wet grass!" Tom shouted.

Then a great, rushing coolness burst over Jenny. She fell headlong into darkness and then into light. She hit something hard and unyielding, and she and Tom were rolling.

They were through.

She was on the floor of Zach's garage. The concrete felt as cold as ice, and she pressed her cheek against it. She stretched her whole body out on it, soaking up the blessed chill. She wanted to kiss it.

Instead, she scrambled to one elbow and looked at Tom. The garage light was on; she could see him. He was all right, his eyes just opening, his chest heaving. She kissed him.

"We did it," he whispered, staring at the ceiling, then at her. His voice was awed. "We did it. We're actually alive."

"I know! I know!" She hugged and kissed him

217

again, in an agony of joyous affection. "We're alive! We're alive!" She was wildly exhilarated. She'd never known how good it was to be alive until she thought she was dying.

Tom was shaking his head. "But I mean—it was impossible. Nobody could have lived through that fire."

"Tom—" She stopped and stared at him. "But, Tom—it was an illusion. You knew that—didn't you?"

"Uh." He gazed around, then puffed his cheeks sheepishly, for a moment looking like Michael. "Actually, no."

"You didn't *believe* me?"

"Well—"

"Then why did you go *with* me?"

He looked at her, then, with eyes that were green and gold and brown like autumn leaves swirling on a pool. "I wanted to," he said simply. "Whatever happened, I wanted to be with you."

Jenny just stared at him a moment. Thunderstruck. Then she whispered. "Oh, Tom!"

And then she was in his arms, sobbing breathlessly. Just his name, over and over. She thought her heart would burst.

I could have lost him. I could have lost him forever. All his brave goodness—all his love for me. I could have lost him . . . I could have lost myself in Julian's darkness.

Never again, she thought fiercely to herself, clinging to Tom as if something were trying to rip her away. The shadows have no power over me anymore. It was as if the fire, the great cleansing fire, had scorched all the dark thoughts out of her. Burning away the part of her that had responded to Julian, that had craved his danger and wildness. Taking that part like a sacrifice. Now that Jenny had come through the fire, she felt purified—renewed. A phoenix reborn.

But the strength that she'd gained from fighting Julian was still with her—that hadn't changed. She was stronger than ever since she'd come through the fire. And she could love Tom more because of her strength. They were equals. They could stand side by side, neither eclipsing the other.

And she knew now that she could trust him to the end. She only hoped he knew the same thing about her—or that she could prove it to him. She was happy to spend the next few decades trying.

Tom's grip on her hand changed. He'd been holding it bruisingly hard; now he turned it over and pulled back to look.

Jenny lifted her head from his shoulder.

"It's gone," Tom said wonderingly. "The ring."

"Of course," Jenny said and nipped his chin. Nothing could surprise her now. Everything was going to be all right. "It's gone—because we won. I'm free. Know anybody who wants one girlfriend, low maintenance, good sense of humor?"

"God, Jenny." His arms tightened rushingly. "Nope, guess you'll have to put an ad in the classifieds," he said into her hair. "Oh, Thorny, I love you."

"You must, you called me Thorny," Jenny said, blinking away tears. "I love you, too, Tommy. For always and always."

Then, in the midst of her euphoria, she thought of something.

"We've got to get the others, you know—oh, my God!" She had just looked at the mural photograph on the wall.

It was on fire.

"You stay here!" Tom was on his feet, whipping off his jacket. He reached for the metal handle of the door in the picture unerringly.

"I'm coming with you!" Jenny shouted back. She grabbed his hand as he pulled on the handle. "You never go anywhere without me again—"

The darkness snatched them up, sucked them in. Deposited them in fire.

It wasn't as bad this time. Jenny put her head down, clung to Tom's hand, and made her legs run. It'll be over in a minute, she told herself as the agony surrounded her. Over in a minute, over in a minute—

Then it *was* over. Cool air was around them. Dee, Zach, Audrey, and Michael were in a row, staring at them, reaching out to catch them as they tumbled in.

"You see?" Jenny gasped to Dee, who was nearest. "All in your mind."

"Oh, God, you're alive!" Dee's hug bruised like Tom's.

"Not a very original observation," Tom said. "Now, look, here's the deal. It's hot and it hurts, but it doesn't kill you. You count about to ten and you're through. Okay?"

Only ten? Jenny thought, sagging a little in Dee's arms. "It feels like a hundred," she confided to Dee's shoulder.

"Think 'cool, wet grass,'" Tom said. "Like

firewalkers do. Keep thinking and keep going and you'll be okay."

Dee nodded. "Let's do it!"

But Michael's eyes were wide and uneasy, and Audrey recoiled a step. Zach remained very still, looking at Jenny. Then he let out his breath.

"Okay," he said. "It's just an illusion. Unreality, here we come."

"Hurry up, *move*," Tom said to the others. "We have to get out before this damn photograph burns up. Who knows *what* happens then." He grabbed Michael by the sweatshirt, then took firm hold of his hand. He held out his other hand to Dee.

Jenny grabbed Audrey.

"No!" Audrey screamed. "I don't want to—"

"That way!" Tom shouted to Michael. "Go on! Straight ahead!" He gave Michael a push that sent him stumbling forward. Dee reached behind her to grab Audrey's hand and pull her along. Jenny shoved Audrey on from behind and held out her free hand to Zach. She felt his thin strong fingers close over it. She felt heat billow up around her.

Then it was like a wild game of crack-the-whip, with everyone surging and running and pulling— and Audrey, at least, trying to pull in the wrong direction. Fire filled Jenny's eyes and ears. She tried to count to ten, but it was impossible—her whole mind was occupied with the struggle of keeping Audrey going forward.

Fire and pain and heat and yanking on her arms—

Then Zach stumbled.

Jenny didn't know how it happened. Her hand was suddenly empty. She groped wildly with it and found nothing. She turned her head, looking frantically behind her. For an instant she thought she saw a black silhouette in the orange inferno, then the flames blotted it out.

Zach . . .

She opened her mouth to scream, and burning air filled her lungs. She choked. She was being pulled forward. There was nothing she could do—unless she let go of Audrey. She was being dragged along. Zach was far behind now.

Then she burst out into coolness and fell.

She landed on top of Audrey. Audrey was whimpering. Jenny was still choking, unable to get her breath.

She was so hot and exhausted and sore. Everything hurt. Her ears were ringing. Her eyes and nose stung, and when she tried to get up, her legs collapsed under her.

But she was alive. And Audrey was alive, because she was making noise. Michael was alive, coughing and gagging and beating at his smoking clothes. Dee was alive, pounding the concrete and shouting joyously.

Tom was alive, and on his feet. Tall and handsome and stern.

"Where's Zach?"

Jenny's throat was raw. "He let go," she said, almost in a whisper. "He tripped and he let go of my hand—"

Dee's grin collapsed. She stared up at the photo on the wall. Flames were licking out of it.

"I couldn't hold on to him," Jenny said, ashamed. "I couldn't help it. . . ."

"I'll get him," Tom said.

"Are you crazy?" Michael shouted. He broke off,

bending over in a fit of coughing. Then he spat and lifted his head again. "Are you nuts? It'll kill you!"

Audrey had rolled over to look up at the photograph with terrified eyes, her spiky lashes matted together.

"We should get a fire extinguisher—" Dee began.

"No! Not till we get back. It might do something—close the door or something. Just wait for us—we'll be back in a minute."

Jenny swallowed dryly. The fire had been worse this time; it must be getting worse every second.

But Zach. Her gray-eyed cousin. He was lost somewhere in that fire. She couldn't just leave him. . . .

"Oh, God," she sobbed. "Tom, I'm going with you." She tried to get up again, but her legs simply wouldn't obey. She looked down at them in astonishment.

"No!" Tom said. "Dee, take care of her!"

"Tom—" Jenny screamed.

"I'll be back. I promise."

He was reaching into the picture—pulling the handle. Then he simply disappeared. The flames shot out and seemed to grab him like hungry hands, snatching him inside. He was gone—and the photograph was ablaze.

Every inch of it was burning now, flames bursting up and fanning out. Leaping so high that at any other time Jenny would have been terrified at the mere sight, afraid for Zach's house. She'd never seen an uncontrolled fire this high.

At this moment all she cared about was the photograph. The entire picture was on fire, blackening and peeling. The image was fading under the flames.

"No!" she screamed. "Tom! *Tom!*"

"We've got to get water!" Dee shouted.

"No! He said not to . . . oh, Tom!"

It was burning. Burning up. Burning out of all recognition. Turning into a black curling mess. The pyramid of tables disappearing as flames licked over them. The door was gone now. The Exit sign was gone.

"Tommeeeeeee!"

Dee's strong hands held her back, keeping her from trying to jump into the photograph. It was no use anyway. There was no handle sticking out of the picture any longer. There was nothing left at all.

The flames began to die as the last of the photo was consumed. Bits of it fell off. Other bits floated in the air, drifting down slowly. Sparks danced upward.

Then it was just a charred and smoldering rectangle on the wall.

Jenny fell to her knees, hands over her face. She hadn't known she could make sounds like that.

"Jenny, don't. Don't. Oh, God, Jenny, please stop." Dee was crying, too, dripping tears down her neck. Dee, who never cried. Audrey crawled up on the other side, wrapping her arms around both of them. They were all sobbing.

"Look, you guys—you guys, don't," Michael gasped. Jenny felt a new pair of arms around her, trying to shake all of them. "Jenny—Jenny, it might not be so bad. He might have made it through. If he made it through to the cafeteria, he's okay."

Jenny couldn't stop sobbing, but she raised her head a little. Michael's face was grimy and anxious and deadly earnest.

"Let's just think about this. It took more than ten

seconds for that picture to burn up. And he could go faster without all of us to hold him back. So he probably *did* make it through—and that means at least he's alive."

There was a shaking in Jenny's middle. "But—but Zach—"

"He may have made it back, too," Michael said desperately. "He may be okay."

Jenny looked up at him. The shaking didn't stop, but it lessened. She felt more connected to the world. "Really?" she whispered. "Do you think?"

Just then Dee made an odd sound, as if something had bitten her.

"Look!" she said.

Jenny twisted her neck and followed Dee's gaze to the photograph. Then she hissed and turned around all the way to stare at it.

Letters were appearing on the blackened surface, just as letters had appeared on Michael's window in the unnatural frost. Only these were graceful, looping letters, flowing script that ran along the length of the picture. As if a giant calligraphy brush were painting them on the blackness. They glowed red as coals, and wisps of smoke rose from them as they appeared.

Your friends are with me—in the Shadow World. If you want them, come on a treasure hunt. But remember: If you lose, there's the devil to pay.

"Oh, no," Michael whispered.

"But they're not dead," Audrey said, a little tremulously. The red letters were fading already. "You see, they're not dead. Julian's keeping them to bargain with."

Dee just said, "God."

Jenny, though, sat back on her heels, her hands

225

opening and closing. Working, getting ready for action. She thought of the Shadow World, of the swirling ice and darkness in the closet, and the cruel, ancient, hungry eyes there. Tom was somewhere among those eyes, and so was her cousin.

She knew this—but she wasn't shaking anymore. All her weakness and confusion had evaporated. She had heard the challenge and understood.

She wasn't afraid of Julian now. She was stronger than she had ever been before—stronger than she had known she could be. And she knew what she had to do.

"Right," she said and heard her own voice, clear and cold, like a trumpet. "He wants a new game? He'll get it. I know I can beat him now."

"Jenny—" Michael began, looking at her fearfully.

Jenny shook her head, straightened her shoulders. "I can beat him," she said again with complete confidence. To the smoking photograph, black and empty again, she said, *"En garde,* Julian. It's not over till it's over."

About the Author

LISA JANE SMITH realized she wanted to be a writer sometime between kindergarten and first grade. She got the idea for her first published book while baby-sitting in high school, and wrote it while attending college at the University of California at Santa Barbara (in between classes, of course).

Dreams and nightmares have always fascinated her. Many of her books, including *The Forbidden Game* trilogy, are based on her own nightmares and those of her friends. At times she stops in the middle of a particularly frightening dream and thinks, "This is awful. I sure hope I remember it when I wake up!"

She lives in a rambling house in the Bay Area of northern California with one dog, three cats, and about ten thousand books.

THE
FORBIDDEN GAME

continues...
Look out for Book 3:
THE KILL

Play at your own risk...

Jenny may have escaped, but the Shadow World has kept two of her friends. The last game will either free them all for good, or ensure they never, *ever* leave. . .

Point Horror

Are you hooked on horror? Are you thrilled by fear? Then these are the books for you. A powerful series of horror fiction designed to keep you quaking in your shoes.

Titles available now:

The Cemetery
D.E. Athkins

The Dead Game
Mother's Helper
A. Bates

The Cheerleader
The Return of the Vampire
The Vampire's Promise
Freeze Tag
The Perfume
The Stranger
Twins
Caroline B. Cooney

April Fools
The Lifeguard
The Mall
Teacher's Pet
Trick or Treat
Richie Tankersley Cusick

Camp Fear
My Secret Admirer
Silent Witness
The Window
Carol Ellis

The Accident
The Invitation
The Fever
Funhouse
The Train
Nightmare Hall:
The Silent Scream
Deadly Attraction
The Roommate
The Wish
Guilty
Diane Hoh

The Yearbook
Peter Lerangis

The Watcher
Lael Littke

The Forbidden Game:
The Hunter
The Chase
L.J. Smith

Dream Date
The Diary
The Waitress
Sinclair Smith

The Phantom
Barbara Steiner

The Baby-sitter
The Baby-sitter II
The Baby-sitter III
Beach House
Beach Party
The Boyfriend
Call Waiting
The Dead Girlfriend
The Girlfriend
Halloween Night
The Hitchhiker
Hit and Run
The Snowman
The Witness
R.L. Stine

Thirteen Tales of Horror
Various
Thirteen More Tales of Horror
Various
Thirteen Again
Various

Look out for:

Nightmare Hall:
The Scream Team
Diane Hoh

The Forbidden Game III:
The Kill
L.J. Smith

Fatal Secrets
Richie Tankersley Cusick

Point Romance

If you like Point Horror, you'll love Point Romance!

Are you burning with passion and aching with desire? Then these are the books for you! Point Romance brings you passion, romance, heartache, . . . and *love*.

Available now:

First Comes Love:
To Have and to Hold
For Better, For Worse
In Sickness and in Health
Till Death Do Us Part
Last Summer, First Love:
A Time to Love
Goodbye to Love
Jennifer Baker

A Winter Love Story
Jane Claypool Miner

Two Weeks in Paradise
Spotlight on Love
Denise Colby

Saturday Night
Last Dance
New Year's Eve
Summer Nights
Caroline B. Cooney

Cradle Snatcher
Kiss Me, Stupid
Alison Creaghan

Summer Dreams, Winter Love
Mary Francis Shura

The Last Great Summer
Carol Stanley

Lifeguards:
Summer's Promise
Summer's End
Todd Strasser

Crazy About You
French Kiss
Robyn Turner

Look out for:

Two-Timer
Lorna Read

Hopelessly Devoted
Amber Vane

Russian Nights
Robyn Turner

Now available from

Point Horror

T-shirts to make you *tremble!*

Want to be the coolest kid in the school? Then mosey on down to your local bookshop and pick up your Point Horror T-shirt and book pack.

Wear if you dare!

T-shirt and book pack available from your local bookshop now.

POINT SF

Encounter worlds where men and women make
hazardous voyages through space; where time travel is a
reality and the fifth dimension a possibility; where the
ultimate horror has already happened and mankind
breaks through the barrier of technology . . .

The Obernewtyn Chronicles:
Book 1: Obernewtyn
Book 2: The Farseekers
Isobelle Carmody
A new breed of humans are born into a hostile world
struggling back from the brink of apocalypse . . .

Random Factor
Jessica Palmer
Battle rages in space. War has been erased from earth and is
now controlled by an all-powerful computer – until a random
factor enters the system . . .

First Contact
Nigel Robinson
In 1992 mankind launched the search for extra-terrestial
intelligence. Two hundred years later, someone responded . . .

Virus
Molly Brown
A mysterious virus is attacking the staff of an engineering plant
. . . Who, or *what* is responsible?

Look out for:

Strange Orbit
Margaret Simpson

Scatterlings
Isobelle Carmody

Body Snatchers
Stan Nicholls

Read Point SF and enter a new dimension . . .